SHOUT OUT

USE YOUR VOICE

SAVE THE DAY!

Published in the UK by Scholastic Children's Books, 2021
Euston House, 24 Eversholt Street, London, NW1 1DB, UK
Unit 89E, Lagan Road, Dublin Industrial Estate, Glasnevin, Dublin 11
A division of Scholastic Limited.

London – New York – Toronto – Sydney – Auckland
Mexico City – New Delhi – Hong Kong

Text © Roman Kemp and Vick Hope, 2021
Illustrations by Jason Cockcroft © Scholastic Children's Books, 2021

ISBN 978 1407 19691 6

A CIP catalogue record for this book
is available from the British Library.

Printed and bound by CPI Group (UK) Ltd, Croydon, CR0 4YY
Papers used by Scholastic Children's Books are made
from wood grown in sustainable forests.

SCHOLASTIC

ROMAN KEMP & VICK HOPE

SHOUT OUT

In collaboration with
CHLOE SEAGER

Illustrated by
JASON COCKCROFT

CHAPTER ONE

[INTRO: *Radio Royalty* jingle (5 secs).]

ARTHUR: IT'S MATCH DAY! And the atmosphere is *tense* ...

KIERAN: That's right, Arthur! Fans on both sides are chanting already, as the players file off the coach. But the big question on everyone's mind is ... will Victory Road *finally* be able to put a stop to their losing streak against Summerby?!

ARTHUR: That's right, Kieran! Well, we at *Radio Royalty* could not be more excited to find out ...

KIERAN: Arthur got so excited he tripped over and nearly injured one of the players.

ARTHUR: *Awkward laughter* Unbelievable scenes, Kieran! I mean ... that's not *exactly* what happened ...

It is *what happened*, thought Arthur, but Kieran didn't have to *literally* broadcast it to the entire school! A pitfall of running one of the most popular radio shows in the school was definitely that sometimes your most embarrassing moments were laid bare for everyone to hear. Arthur didn't fall over because he was overexcited about the game, though; it was ... well. Maybe it was better if everyone thought that *was* the reason. The *actual* reason was because Arthur was staring at a girl.

Not just "a girl". A new friend. Whose name was Anna. Anna the girl friend. No, not *girlfriend*!! Girl who was a friend ... like Grace! Anna, who went to their rival school, Summerby Secondary. Anna, who he'd met on the shared Victory Road/Summerby Secondary coach that morning, en route to the big Summerby versus Victory Road football game. Anna, who he'd laughed and joked around with the whole journey, and who had made him laugh out loud thirteen times (Arthur had been counting). Anna, who smelled like coconut mixed with lemons.

Arthur shook his head. They'd arrived at Greenfair Park now, and he really needed to snap out of it. He hoped beyond hope that this game would go better than their last against Summerby, which Arthur and Kieran had both played in. They had lost three-nil, which hardly *ever* happened. Kieren was their star striker and he usually always got at least one goal. It was weird, but ... it was almost like Summerby knew whenever he was going to shoot.

Maybe the boys' team *had* been playing too predictably. That was why, for today's game – the girls' match – the team had decided to shake up their tactics. Whereas they usually played in a four-four-two formation, today they'd gone for a surprise five-three-two.

3

Arthur watched Grace Best limbering up. She was staring straight ahead at the other team, eyes not wavering as she stretched one leg while balancing perfectly on the other. Arthur would never admit it to Grace, but even though they were friends, he was still a little intimidated by her. He definitely wouldn't want to be on the Summerby team, anyway. Grace was a winger for Victory Road and a key part of their "surprise" tactics. Whereas in the old formation she would run up and down the wing, attacking like a mad thing, this time she would cut inside, allowing the left back to run around her and score.

The team had gone over and over their new strategy back at Victory Road. They *needed* the win after so many recent losses to their neighbouring school, and Arthur couldn't *wait* to commentate and broadcast their inevitable triumph on their school radio station, *Listen Up!*

"Shall we interview the teams?" Kieran suggested, shaking Arthur from his thoughts.

Arthur squared his shoulders. "Let's do it." He wasn't distracted by his new girl ... friend ... friend-girl ... any more. He was *focused*.

They headed across the park, towards the Victory Road team. The sun was shining, glimmering across the pond, and the air smelled of fresh-cut grass. It was the perfect day for a lively game. Arthur tried not to think about the plans that had been announced to build a luxury block of flats right here. It had been a complete shock for everyone in the area, and there was a big protest planned to save the park. Everyone had high hopes that the council would listen to them.

As they approached, Grace was still balancing on one leg and staring stony-eyed at the Summerby team. She gave a quick nod in greeting and then went back to eyeballing her competitors. The other girls were whispering to each other, going over their strategy one last time. You could feel the nervous, excited energy in the air.

Amongst the girls was Misha Klimach, who Arthur, Kieran and Grace knew well. She was instructing the rest of the team while pulling her arm behind her head to warm up. It was funny to think that this was the same Misha from last term. Misha used to hide in her sister Nikita's shadow. She was super good at maths, science and chess, but always came second best to Nikita. When the coveted chess trophy went missing in the *middle of a tournament*, it had turned out to be Misha who had stolen it, longing to shine on her own for once. Arthur, Kieran and Grace's stellar investigative journalism had revealed the truth . . . but in the end, they decided not to tell everyone because Misha was truly sorry and desperate to make amends.

Looking at her now, Arthur was surer than ever that the trio had made the right call. Sitting on that kind of scoop was painful and went against every journalistic bone in his body, but if they'd told everyone, Misha might never have ended up where she was now: laughing and smiling in amongst a new group of friends, and known all around school for putting endless balls in the back of the net. She'd be the perfect person for their first interview. Arthur nudged Kieran and they stepped towards her with their trusty microphone, Mikey.

And they weren't the only ones. Almost like she could smell that an interview was afoot, Grace snapped out of her focused pre-game trance and headed towards the boys and Misha.

But Arthur put his hand out in front of her. "Grace. We've been over this. You can't cover the match for *Best of the Best* because you're *in the match*."

Best of the Best was Grace's radio show and, much to Arthur and Kieran's constant annoyance, it was every bit as popular as their show, *Radio Royalty*.

"Thanks for the physics lesson, Arthur," said Grace, folding her arms. "I just thought you might need some help from a pro."

As burns went, it was a solid seven out of ten, but Arthur just smirked. Grace Best and Arthur McLean used to be the *biggest* enemies – everyone at school knew it. And, from the outside, it might seem as though they still were. But now they were solid frenemies, and Arthur knew Grace's jibes were all in jest. Life without their competitive banter would be dull as.

"If you want to pick up some tips for your next interview, sure," Arthur replied. "Come on then, Bestie."

Grace scowled, but she followed him and Kieran anyway. Except, just as they approached

Misha with their microphone outstretched, another microphone shot in front of her face.

"So, Misha," said a voice. "Thanks for agreeing to chat with us. *Anna's Amusings* listeners are keen to hear about your *incredible* rise to football fame. But the question we're all truly wondering is . . . how *do* you get that perfect sock-to-knee ratio?"

There was a burst of laughter from the crowd surrounding Misha. Kieran nudged Arthur. "Arthur, isn't that . . .?"

But Arthur had already realized. And he was frozen on the spot.

It was *Anna*. Bus girl Anna.

Her long, dark hair was swept up in a ponytail. She stood with her feet apart and shoulders back, oozing confidence. She was clearly revelling in the laughs she was getting from the bystanders. In his head, Arthur went over the conversation they'd had. Did she mention that she did radio too?! Arthur was *sure* he would have remembered . . .

"I didn't know she was Anna Fong, as in *Anna's Amusings* Anna!" Kieran went on, as Anna cracked another joke. A whole grinning crowd had gathered around her now. "I've heard about her show from my cousin who goes to Summerby. Mate . . . she's *funny*."

Arthur's mouth dried up. She made him nervous enough already, and now she was a fellow funny radio presenter?

Just then a dictaphone waved in front of Misha's face. "Notes for *Summerby Stories* coverage of Victory Road versus Summerby Secondary girls' match. Interview with Misha Klimach, Victory Road star striker."

A well-groomed, smart-looking boy was nodding at Misha, who wasn't sure where to look. Arthur noticed straight away that he had an air of authority. People around him were going quiet and straightening up. They clearly took him seriously.

"Well, well, well," muttered Grace. "If it isn't *Michael Bernard*. If I'd have known *Summerby Stories* were covering the match, I'd have warned our team to hide in the changing rooms before the game."

"Who?!" Arthur asked. "How do you guys know all this?"

Grace and Kieran looked at him with raised eyebrows. And it wasn't often Kieran raised an eyebrow.

"You've never heard of *Anna's Amusings* or *Summerby Stories*?" Grace chided. "Arthur, you really need to research your competition. *Anna's Amusings* is the most listened-to radio show at Summerby, and Michael is the editor of *Summerby Stories*, their student newspaper."

"They don't even go to our school!" Arthur cried. "They're *not* my competition."

"They are today," Grace replied.

Arthur looked across at Anna and Michael, who were squaring up to each other. Michael had his arms folded defensively, and Anna was nonchalantly rolling up her sleeves, as if Michael butting into her interview didn't bother her at all. Clearly journalistic rivalry was just as fierce at Summerby as it was at Victory Road.

Michael wasn't the only one with his arms folded – Grace was at it too. "God, they're so annoying," she said, narrowing her eyes at them. "How *dare* they move in on Misha. They should interview their own team!"

"We can take them," said Arthur, as he rolled up his sleeves.

"Erm, guys," said Kieren, as his eyes moved between Grace and Arthur, and Michael and Anna. "Do they . . . remind you of anyone?"

"Can't think." Arthur shrugged.

Kieran's eyes were disbelieving.

"Arthur, Kieren, get in there!" Grace hollered. "They're stealing your interview!"

Michael was shooting intense, quick-fire questions at poor Misha, who barely had time to think about her answer before he asked her another. Meanwhile, Anna was doubled over laughing about one of the players' last names being "Weenus".

Together they approached Michael, Anna and Misha. When Anna spotted Arthur, she stopped laughing and gave a small smile. Arthur cringed as he noticed his heart starting to beat way faster. And it wasn't anticipation for the match.

"Well, well, well," Michael muttered. "If it isn't *Grace Best*. If I'd have known you were coming, I'd have bought our team some noise-cancelling headphones."

"To block out the sound of us beating you?" Grace retorted, quick as anything.

Arthur smirked. He enjoyed Grace's comebacks when they weren't being turned on *him*. And he was glad Grace was as sharp as ever, because his own tongue seemed to be completely tied in Anna's presence.

"We'll see about that," Michael returned.

There was a tense stand-off, as the five journalists stood in rows, eyeballing each other. Anna and Michael on one side, Arthur, Kieran and Grace facing them. Misha took the opportunity to slip away.

"Shouldn't you be warming up your legs instead of your tongue, Grace," Anna said, "and leave the interviews to the presenters actually covering the event?"

Arthur's eyebrows flew up his forehead. Brutal! This was a different side to the jokey, lighthearted girl he had met on the bus. He wondered if Anna had known who *he* was when they'd spoken. She *must* have done, because she didn't seem at all surprised to see him with a microphone now.

Grace's fists curled at Anna's comment. No matter how much she enjoyed being on the pitch, Arthur could tell that she was hating having to relinquish her microphone.

"Look, look," said Kieran, ever the diplomat, as he put his hands out between everyone. "We're all here for the same thing. Can we all agree to take turns, yeah?"

"Sure, sounds like a good plan," Michael

replied. "And you guys can go *last*."

Grace opened her mouth to yell something, but before she could speak a loud whistle interrupted. The match was starting.

"Victory Road is going to *crush* Summerby," she said. "*And* we're going to get better coverage. Everyone knows the winning team always gets the most listeners."

"I admire your confidence ..." Anna said, and for a minute Arthur wondered if she was really complimenting them. But then she added, "... for a school that has lost their last three games."

"Oh, you are *on*," Grace shouted as she ran off to join the rest of the team, who were lining up on the pitch.

"I hope your presenting skills are better than your comebacks, Arthur," Anna winked.

"Yeah ... well ... that would be rising to bite ... I mean *bait!*" Arthur fumbled. "I don't bite . . . obviously."

Arthur felt himself start to blush. What was *wrong* with him?! Why was he tripping over his words?

Anna was smiling. "Well, thank you for clarifying that you don't bite. But you'll need to up your game if you're going to stand a chance against us in the Park Protests contest," she added.

Kieran and Arthur looked at each other. "The *what*?"

"Don't tell me you haven't heard!" Anna tutted. "Boys, boys, not a good start . . ." She reached in her bag for a crumpled flyer and handed it to Arthur, lightly brushing his hand. Not that he noticed.

With a swish of her ponytail, Anna followed Michael to sit with the other Summerby supporters while Kieran and Arthur hurriedly smoothed out the creased bit of paper.

PARK PROTESTS
YOUNG JOURNALIST CONTEST

DREAMING OF A CAREER IN JOURNALISM?

THEN THIS IS THE OPPORTUNITY FOR YOU!

Greenfair FM 96.3 and *Greenfair Weekly* are coming together in the search for an aspiring young journalist to cover the much-anticipated "Save Greenfair Park" protests on 27th March

THE PRIZE:

The winner will help to cover the park protests in print and broadcast, with the support of experienced journalists from *Greenfair FM* and *Greenfair Weekly*.

Not only will the winning journalist help spread the important message of the protests, but this will be a once-

in-a-lifetime opportunity to kickstart
their career.

THE RULES

This competition is open to Greenfair
residents between nine and fourteen years
of age. No prior media experience is
required to enter. Entries must consist of
three written or recorded pieces published
or broadcast/aired no more than two
months prior to the closing date.
Entries must be submitted by 12 p.m. on
April 17th.

Arthur's pulse started racing. This was ...
unbelievable. An opportunity to be broadcast
not only on school radio, but *actual radio*.

"Arthur!" Kieran began shaking him. "This
is incredible! They must want a local kid to help
pull at community heartstrings, or something.

Oh, when Grace sees this . . ."

Grace would be giving this everything she had and, clearly, so would Anna and Michael. Arthur thought back to earlier, when he'd said *Anna's Amusings* and *Summerby Stories* weren't his competition. It seemed that wasn't the case any more.

Kieran patted Arthur's shoulder. "Come on, mate, more on this later. We've got to get our heads in the game. Victory Road for the win!"

CHAPTER TWO

[INTRO: *Best of the Best* jingle (7 secs).]

GRACE: I'm Grace Best, bringing you your live travel update. A blockage involving a lorry becoming separated from its cargo on the North Circular at the M1 junction has meant serious bottlenecking. Long delays are involved for everyone caught in the mile-long tailback ...

Grace tried to distract herself by using Arthur's mic to record a travel report on the bus home, but it was no good. She couldn't pretend to be upbeat when the Victory Road girls had lost yet again. She couldn't even focus properly on the *amazing* news about the park protests competition, which was basically the opportunity of her dreams!

Ugh, *why* did Summerby and Victory Road have to share a bus?! She tried to drown out the victory song of the Summerby team. *So* obnoxious. Grace would *never* be such a bad winner ... probably. To make things even worse they had been stuck in a traffic jam for an hour now, and the Summerby singing showed no signs of relenting.

Grace had been stewing over the game the whole journey. If there was anything she hated, it was losing ... but she *especially* hated losing when it wasn't fair! She had been so sure their plan was foolproof. Victory Road had *never* used tactics like that before. How had Summerby been able to defend so well? It was almost like ... they'd anticipated them?!

Loud laughter penetrated her moody bubble.

It was Arthur and Anna. How could he be having banter with a Summerby student at a time like this? Traitorous toad.

"Cheer up, Grace," Arthur called across to her. "It's a shame we lost, but you played brilliantly."

Grace smiled, feeling slightly better. "Thanks Arthur, I ..." she began to reply, but he'd already turned back towards Anna, distracted by her impression of a manatee. (She managed to make her cheeks HUGE and her expression was spot on, but that was so not the point.) Arthur clearly cared more about doing animal impressions with his *new friend* than he did about Victory Road's dignity.

It had all started off brilliantly. The team's energy was high. They were sure that their new and unexpected strategy would work, and they were dominating the field. Misha scored an *amazing* early goal, heading the ball straight into the net after a killer pass from Lia. The Victory Road supporters whooped. She could hear Kieran and Arthur yelling, "SHE SHOOTS, SHE SCORES!" and Grace had fallen to her knees in celebration, believing that everything was coming together. She could *feel* it. They were finally going to end their losing streak against Summerby.

And then it all went horribly wrong.

The plan was that Grace, who usually ran up and down the wing, would play centrally. She would cut inside to allow the wing-back, Lia, to go around her and shoot. But, weirdly, it was like the defence knew *exactly* what they were going to do. Players who would never normally mark Lia were suddenly on her tail. And players who would usually mark Grace were abruptly disinterested. Lia couldn't get anywhere *near* the goal. Everyone was so thrown off they didn't score again, and Summerby went on to score twice.

Grace ground her teeth. Either the Summerby team were able to shift tactics ridiculously quickly after seeing their new five-three-two formation, or . . .

A terrible idea started to take shape in her mind: *someone* had snitched on what they planned to do, and Summerby were prepared. Grace always trusted her journalistic instincts, and in this instance she smelled a rat.

"Are you OK, Grace?" asked Lia. She was sitting in front of Grace, but leaned over and patted her on the shoulder. Lia's friend Tilly-Mae, who was a Summerby student and sitting beside Lia, also bobbed her head over the seat.

"Chin up . . ." Tilly-Mae gave a sympathetic look. "Imagine being a camel without a hump."

Grace wrinkled her nose. "Huh?"

"She means things could be worse," Lia translated, giving Tilly-Mae's arm an affectionate squeeze. "We've lived next door for

25

so many years now . . ." she added. "You learn to speak Tilly-Mae eventually."

Tilly-Mae grinned and turned away. Grace tried to smile at Lia, even though she'd barely said two words to anyone and eaten an entire Tupperware full of her mum's homemade chin-chin.

"Sometimes it's just not meant to be. But hey, next time!"

Lia's head disappeared. She was such a nice girl, thought Grace. A "real team player", as their coach called her. Grace smiled and let a momentary warmth flow through her. Even if they had lost, she was still happy to be here with the squad. She'd been nervous to get to know them all at first – she was so used to spending time with her brothers, or with Arthur and Kieran, that the huge group of girls seemed intimidating. But day by day they became less scary, and she was loving the perks of mates who you could borrow a hair bobble from, or who would make you feel better about your giant spot by pointing out their own rather than laughing at it. But how well did she *really* know them? Grace looked around at her fellow students. She felt certain that all their recent, inexplicable losses to Summerby weren't a coincidence. It just didn't make any sense! *Someone* from Victory Road was feeding Summerby information, so there had to be two culprits involved: a mole and whoever they were reporting back to ...

Grace eyeballed the back of Lia and Tilly-Mae's heads with new suspicion. Lia was nice. But was she *too nice*? She was such good friends with everyone ... including this Summerby girl, Tilly-Mae. Everyone knew they went way back ... their mums went to pre-natal group together and now they lived next door. Lia being able to translate Tilly-Mae's kooky way of speaking meant they must be super tight, *and* she heard that Lia once lent Tilly-Mae her prized lucky pen ... What other favours might she be doing for her?!

She watched Lia and Tilly-Mae whispering conspiratorially and plaiting each other's hair. Tilly-Mae gasped at something Lia said. Just *what* was Lia sharing? Was Tilly-Mae taking advantage of Lia's open, kind-hearted nature? Or was her "nice girl" persona all an act?

"Excellent control of the ball today, Grace," said a voice from the other side of the coach. It was fellow Victory Road student, Diaz ... sitting next to Michael of *Summerby Stories*. It hadn't occurred to Grace before, but now that she thought about it, *why* was he here? He *never* usually took an interest in school sports, so didn't have an *actual* reason to be there, beyond "moral support". It was dubious to say the least.

"Thanks, Diaz," Grace replied. As he turned

back, she fixed her gaze on his profile. What information did she have on Diaz, apart from the fact he was head of the Victory Road debate club ... What was with his sudden interest in girls' football? And his best friend was a Summerby student! In fact, now that she thought about it, she rarely saw Diaz with any pals at Victory Road. Apart from other members of the debate team, which seemed more of a business-like relationship. Was Michael his only friend? How far would he be willing to go for him?

Michael was clearly the serious, silent type. But Grace didn't know much about him either, apart from that he was smart and incredibly competitive, so from what she knew she wouldn't put anything past him. Michael seemed to be quite the loner, too, apart from his friendship with Diaz. They were prime suspects, for sure.

Finally, Grace's gaze landed on Arthur and

Anna, who were still laughing maniacally at the back of the bus. What did any of them really know about Arthur's new friend? Apart from the fact she was a rival! She didn't tell him who she was, which was suspicious to say the least. And they had become chummy *very* quickly – almost like she'd singled Arthur out, with some sort of plan in mind. What if she was using him? Arthur was a trusting soul. He may accidentally let something slip without even realizing.

The strangest thing, though, was that all these leaks had happened at different events. They'd lost the last two boys' games, their last netball match, hockey match, the inter-school Bake Off – even the inter-school chess tournament, which Victory Road were usually the best at! And who had won every single inter-school fixture that she could think of over the past two months?

Summerby.

But who could have a motive to want Summerby to win everything? Surely no Summerby student is on *every single team*? And could all that information be coming from a singular source? Or, even worse, were there *multiple* informants? Who knew how deep this ran or how high up it went?

Grace wasn't sure of her theory yet, but one way or another she was certain there was something amiss. Perhaps she should take it to a teacher or parent. But who would believe her? She could hear it now ... "Be a gracious loser, Grace." "You're imagining things, Grace." Plus, she couldn't help but think, with a twinkle, that there was a scoop to be found here. This wasn't just straightforward cheating like the theft of the trophy was – this was cheating across different sports, teams and clubs ... across *schools*. Imagine! What would it be like to expose something that big?

Finally, after what felt like a year, they pulled into the Victory Road High School grounds. Grace jumped up from her seat with relief and a newfound vigour. She watched Lia hugging Tilly-Mae, and Diaz fist-bumping Michael, and Arthur awkwardly going in for a hug with Anna and then changing his mind and patting her on the head. (So awkward.)

Surveying the Summerby Secondary students left on the coach, ready to be driven down the road back to their own school, Grace *knew* that someone here was an underhanded crook. And she was going to find out who. She couldn't wait to talk to Arthur and Kieran later.

Grace felt another investigation coming on, and she couldn't do it alone.

CHAPTER THREE

SUMMERBY *STORIES*

NEWS : SPORTS : ENTERTAINMENT : INTERVIEWS AND MORE

SUMMERBY SLAMS VICTORY ROAD

Despite a shock change in tactics Victory Road lose yesterday's match, as Michael Bernard reports for Summerby Stories

After an early goal only ten minutes into the game, it looked as if Victory Road had it in the bag when, in an unusual move, Victory Road's winger, Grace Best, cut inside as wing-back Lia Diakos sprinted down the side. Her pledge to score was, however, thwarted, as just moments later, Diakos found herself tackled from behind by Summerby player Tilly-Mae Hewson. Hewson's impeccable swipe put Summerby firmly back in possession of the ball, and she went on to score a spectacular goal for Summerby, which ultimately cost Victory Road the game.

"Are you sure you're not just a bad loser, Grace?" Arthur ribbed, after the fourth time rereading *Summerby Stories'* coverage of the match, which Grace had pulled up online.

"I'm telling you!" Grace squealed. "They knew before the match! How else could they possibly have responded to our new formation that fast? If it was just once, then *maybe*. But how do you explain all the other times we've lost in the last two months? Kieran didn't even get a single goal at our last game with them! When was the last time you *didn't* score a goal, Kieran, before that?"

Kieran scratched his head. "Um . . ."

"Exactly, see! He can't even remember!" Grace sat back triumphantly, as if this proved everything.

"It *was* odd," Kieran conceded. "It was like they always knew where I was going to be. I figured we were just being super predictable and they'd upped their game."

"The last Summerby match you played before that, you won three-nil. It's a bit of a quick turnaround, isn't it?!" Grace prodded.

"It is, but—" Arthur started.

"—And look!" Grace interrupted, pulling up a table of sports results online. "These are the match results of the past year. Summerby Secondary versus Victory Road High. It's a pretty even spread of wins and losses. Except, of course, when Kieran's playing football, in which case we usually win."

Kieran grinned.

"And then since two months ago, BOOM. Look at Victory. Lose, lose, lose, lose, lose."

Arthur and Kieran studied the table. "I do see what you're saying," Arthur admitted. "It just seems so unlikely ..."

"What's *unlikely*," said Grace, pulling up another of Michael's *Summerby Stories* articles, "is both teams baking the same cake at the Bake Off, only Summerby added five extra cherries, pipping us to the post. Coincidence?"

Arthur and Michael peered at Michael's article, and the picture of the two nearly identical cakes.

"That *is* weird ..." admitted Arthur. "But who would be leaking information about all these different contests? Who would have the knowledge? And who would *care* about winning this many different things?"

"I wondered that as well, and I've developed a few theories," Grace answered.

Arthur's stomach knotted. He already guessed what one of Grace's theories might be, because he'd thought the same thing. If the spy was Michael or Anna, they'd have a motive for wanting to win everything. Everyone knew that if their school's team was losing, audience numbers dropped off by about a third, but if they were winning, everyone wanted to tune in, and everyone wanted to read about it the next day. Success sells.

Arthur thought back to their coverage of the game. He and Kieran had struggled to make it entertaining. Lots of people had switched off during the show and no one had listened online afterwards. If your school won everything, it would make your ratings much higher.

But Arthur trusted Anna. Didn't he? I mean . . . sure, she didn't mention who she was when they met, but maybe she just forgot?

"I hate to say it, but Anna and Michael are prime suspects," Grace ventured cautiously. Both she and Kieran side-eyed Arthur to check for his reaction.

"Look, it wasn't Anna, all right? Cross her off the list," Arthur defended.

He thought of the nice message he'd got from her just this morning:

Never thought I'd say this but being stuck in a traffic jam was actually fun! Anna x

Up until now he'd been pleased about it. (Even if he was freaking out. How should he reply? Enthusiastic or play it cool? Kiss or no kiss? What a nightmare.) But now a little bead of sweat ran down his forehead. He couldn't let on to the others, but . . . Well. He *may* have hinted to Anna about the team's new strategy before the game. But she'd sworn to secrecy! There was *no way* she was the mole. She was too nice!

"Look, Arthur, emotions can't get in the way of good journalism," Grace said, in her typical no-nonsense fashion. "Is there *any* way you might have let something slip to Anna?"

Kieran and Grace stared at him. He gulped. If he admitted it now, Anna would rise straight to the top of the suspects list, and he knew in his gut that it wasn't her. So what was the point of telling them?

". . . No," he answered.

Kieran and Grace nodded. Ugh. He felt *awful* for lying. But telling them Anna knew about the team's strategy was only going to point them in the wrong direction and waste all of their time, when they should be finding the *real* culprit.

"All right, well, I didn't see Anna talking to anyone else from Victory Road before the event, which makes Michael more likely, and Diaz his potential stooge," deduced Grace.

"It *was* weird that Diaz was there. I've never seen him at a girls' football match before," Kieran added.

As suspicion diverted away from Anna, Arthur released a breath he'd been holding in.

"I've also been doing some digging on Tilly-Mae Hewson," Grace continued. "She goes to Summerby and is a good friend of none other than Victory Road student Lia Diakos. It looks like she is one of the few girls in *every single society*."

"No way!" Kieran exclaimed. "What ... even baking?"

Grace nodded towards Michael's article on the screen. There, standing behind the winning cake in a line of students, was Tilly-Mae. She was beaming and wearing a chef's hat.

"Who has that much *time*?" Kieran whispered in awe.

"Are there other girls who are on every team?" Arthur asked. "Are they suspects as well?"

"Potentially," Grace replied. "But get this: Tilly-Mae's *brother* is on every single *boys'* team."

Arthur's heart soared with joy. Tilly-Mae and her brother were a member of every team, club and society that Summerby had to offer? Of course they'd want to win everything! And Diaz suddenly showing up at a girls' game that he had nothing to do with? Why would he do that, unless he was feeding info to Michael? Tilly-Mae and Lia, and Michael and Diaz, were *much* more suspicious than Anna!

Grace *was* right. There was something strange going on. Something *big* . . . maybe even bigger than the theft of the chess trophy. Cheating in multiple events, with different schools, involving who knew how many students?! His head was spinning at the thought of it – and the thought of uncovering the truth.

"Why don't we start by talking to Misha?" Kieran suggested. "See if she's seen anything suspicious?"

But Grace was chomping at the bit. "Or we could head straight to Lia?"

Arthur frowned. "I don't know, Grace, last time we rushed in there flinging accusations left, right and centre, it didn't end well. Maybe we should talk to Misha first. See if we can glean any information. After all, she trusts us now."

Grace conceded, even though her number one suspect was probably Anna. Why hadn't Anna mentioned who she was when she first met Arthur? That was just *weird*. Grace didn't trust her, not one bit. But Arthur had closed the door on that line of inquiry. For now.

"All right, go team!" Kieran clapped.

They stood up, ready for action. Grace charged ahead and Arthur smiled. Life was so much more fun when he was working *with* Grace instead of against her. Even if he did still enjoy it when *Radio Royalty* beat *Best of the Best* in the *Listen Up!* school radio ratings.

***

They found Misha hanging out on the benches by the field, surrounded by the other sporty girls in her year. They were sitting in a row, watching one girl doing keepy-uppies, but as soon as Misha saw them coming towards her she stopped counting and her eyes narrowed.

"The sight of you three approaching with a microphone is never good news for me," she said as they neared.

Arthur smiled sheepishly. "We just want

to ask you a few questions ... not about *you*, promise!"

Misha nodded. "OK."

They left the bench and walked to a quiet spot, around the back of the field.

Arthur held the microphone to Misha, and Kieran started the questions. Once he'd made them feel comfortable, and Arthur had put them at ease with a few jokes, Grace would swoop in to tease out the information they needed. The three of them had learned to play to their strengths when working together.

"We just wondered if you saw anything unusual the day of the match?" Grace asked, after they'd chatted with her for a bit.

Misha thought for a second. "Yes, actually." Kieran, Grace and Arthur all leaned in. "One of the girls put peanut butter on her apple as a way of making it more palatable."

Kieran did a double take. "What? Peanut

butter . . . on an apple?"

Misha nodded. "She says it's delicious."

Kieran looked as though his mind had been blown. "I'm going to try it as soon as I get home," he declared.

"Uhh, that *is* unusual . . ." Arthur interjected, "but we were more wondering if there was anything that might lead you to believe someone was passing information to the other team?"

Misha's eyes widened. She was clearly caught off guard. "No. I mean . . . no. Why? Has that happened?"

"That's what we're trying to find out," said Grace.

Misha looked lost in thought. "I don't . . . I mean . . . I love all of my friends. I don't believe anyone would do that."

Grace could see how much Misha was struggling to process what they were implying. Misha had only just made a solid group of friends, who she relied on as part of a team, and now they were raising the idea that one of them might not be trustworthy. It was a lot to take in. Having just started to discover how amazing teamwork could be, Grace was finding it difficult, too.

"OK, well, if you didn't see anything you didn't see anything. We're sorry to have bothered you," said Arthur, and he and Kieran started walking away.

Grace lingered and gave Misha a supportive smile. Misha looked deeply uncomfortable right now, and girls' instinct – which Grace had been honing over the past few months of playing in the football team – told Grace that Misha had something else to say but didn't want to be a snake.

"It's OK, you know, Misha," said Grace. "Telling us what you saw doesn't make you a bad friend or a tell-tale."

Misha took a deep breath. "OK, well . . . I

47

did see Tilly-Mae and Lia whispering about something in the changing room. I thought it was strange, right before the match, when everyone should be getting ready and they'd had plenty of time to catch up earlier in the day. I mean ... they live next door to each other."

Arthur and Kieran turned back with interest. *Bingo*, thought Grace.

"But Lia is so lovely. I can't imagine she'd tell the other team anything! It was probably just about their dance routines for the big talent show next week," Misha garbled. "They talk about it all the time."

Another tasty nugget of information: Tilly-Mae and Lia were always talking about the inter-school talent show. Even though they weren't performing together, but in competing troupes. That seemed fishy ...

"Thanks so much, Misha, this has been

really helpful," Grace said.

"You won't tell anyone I said anything, will you?" Misha asked. "I don't want Lia to think I don't trust her."

"We promise. Our sources are confidential. And we're not going to go accusing anyone of anything. We learned our lesson there."

Misha smirked.

"We're just doing a little digging."

"OK, well, that's all I know. Good luck with the investigation," Misha concluded, and she sprinted off to rejoin her pals.

Grace, Arthur and Kieran looked at each other knowingly. Things had just got a lot more interesting. And Grace had a sneaking suspicion that she knew *exactly* where their investigation should take them next . . .

CHAPTER FOUR

ARTHUR: You're tuned into Listen Up! Arthur McLean reporting live for *Radio Royalty* from Greenfair's Got Talent, an event so popular that this year's tickets sold out in just TWO HOURS. I'm joined by Victory Road student Andy Gupta. You had *quite the rollercoaster* getting yours, right?

ANDY: I mean, yeah, it was crazy. You just kept hitting refresh, and getting nowhere in the queue ... Then my mate Zara told me about some kid — goes by the name of Billet Bill — who'd bought up loads and was selling them at triple the price ...

ARTHUR: So you went for it?

ANDY: It was madness, Arthur. Kids were going

wild for tickets. Fights were breaking out, there were tears over fakes ... It was my last hope.

KIERAN: Just to jump in, we do not condone buying black market tickets. Ms Lyall caught wind of Billet Bill and everyone who purchased from him was refunded the extra money.

ANDY: Yeah, thank god! That was gonna be three months' savings wiped out!

ARTHUR: Well, Andy, tonight's show is set to make it all worthwhile. Let me tell everyone at home who *didn't* manage to get their hands on a ticket, the atmosphere is ELECTRIC ...

Arthur looked around the room. Sometimes he had to work hard to make events sound more exciting than they were, but tonight the atmosphere really *was* electric. The talent show was always the most popular event of the school year, but this time the Victory Road assembly hall was fuller than he'd ever seen it, packed to the brim with kids and parents from all the local schools! Although, everyone knew the *real* competition was between Victory Road and Summerby ... who together made up half of the acts that had made it through.

This year's rush for tickets had been the craziest they'd ever seen. Priority had been given to the relatives of contestants, and after those had been doled out, there simply weren't enough spots to go around for everybody else. Tons of students hadn't managed to get tickets, so they were all tuning in to catch the show.

They were broadcasting, so Arthur, Kieran and Grace were allowed to sit right at the front. Arthur watched as an endless stream of people trooped in and took their seats, wishing he wasn't so close to the entrance. He had developed an unfortunate habit of thinking every short, dark-haired girl who walked in might be Anna, and every time one did he jumped a little in his seat like a jack-in-the-box.

Kieran patted him on the shoulder. "Are you OK, mate? Do you need the bathroom?"

"What? *No!*" Arthur said indignantly.

"Sorry, sorry," Kieran said, raising his hands. "It's just you're shuffling around a lot."

Arthur glanced across at another person he momentarily thought was Anna, but quickly realized it wasn't her at all but actually a small old man with a similar haircut.

Kieran followed his glance to the door. "OH. I see. You're waiting for someone."

"Am not?" Arthur wasn't even convincing himself.

"Look, it's OK, yeah. Just chill out. *Relax.*" Kieran shrugged.

"Good pep talk, thanks," Arthur bristled. It was OK for Kieran. He was always "relaxed" around girls because all he had to do was say one word in Spanish and they all melted.

Forget that, he didn't even have to say *anything* and they melted! Girls instantly liked him and he never had to second-guess himself. Things were different for Arthur, with his non-olive skin, non-flowing hair and normal length eyelashes.

"Arthur McLean, what are you doing here? You're supposed to be in detention. Hand over that microphone."

Detention? Icy fear snaked down Arthur's back and he sprang out of his chair to face the fearsome headmistress Ms Lyall.

He didn't remember doing anything wrong but . . .

"I'm sorry, Ms Lyall . . ."

Except instead of Ms L, there was a loud cackle and Anna's head bobbed into view. "Gotcha! You should have seen your face!" She doubled over with laughter.

Kieran joined in. "Nice one," he

complimented through his snorts. Anna winked at him.

"My impressions have always been ... *spot on*." She said "spot on" in Ms Lyall's voice. It was eerily similar.

Arthur laughed, but inside he was panicking. How much of his and Kieran's conversation had she heard?! Oh *no*. What if she overheard that he was waiting for her? Arthur literally couldn't think of anything more mortifying. He'd rather the whole school saw him in the fluffy, glittery penguin jumper that his mum knitted for him last Christmas.

"See you in a bit," Anna said, and she walked over to the left side of the stage, where a place was reserved for her to set up recording equipment next to Michael. Presumably they were covering the show, too, for the Summerby kids.

"Arthur, you doughnut," Kieran said as she walked away.

"We don't have time for this, you two," Grace snapped. "We've got to be *on high alert*."

Arthur nodded. Grace was right. Summerby had been winning everything for months, likely through nefarious means, and they were here to catch them out, not get tongue-tied around girls.

Eventually the huge audience finished piling in. After a few minutes the lights dimmed and everyone fell quiet. A few hushed, excited whispers rippled through the crowd, and then the familiar *clip, clop* of high-heeled shoes pierced the silence.

"Welcome, everyone, to the tenth annual *Greenfair's Got Talent*," Ms Lyall's voice echoed through the hall. A spotlight shone on her. Her red hair was pulled tightly into a bun, her suit didn't have a single wrinkle and, as she scanned the audience, her expression seemed to say, "No funny business in my school hall," to every single person. The eyes of a few students widened, and Arthur smiled to himself. She *did* seem scary. Until you saw her in her yellow, fluffy dressing gown, like Arthur had last term. He shuddered. Hopefully this term's investigation would not come to that.

Ms Lyall said a few more curt words of welcome and then introduced the first act. There were to be sixteen throughout the night, four from Summerby, four from Victory and eight from other local schools. Everyone knew the spots were tough to come by – all the acts had been through two rounds of auditions already! – so it was going to be a good show.

First was a girl who played the harp so well, it was like she and the instrument were one being. Next up was a kid who called himself "Bendy Boy" and could twist into all sorts of weird shapes. Then was a name that Arthur, Grace and Kieran knew well . . . Jordan Baptiste!

Jordan was a mysterious lone wolf that the trio had trouble pinning down during the trophy investigation last term. He was a slippery fish, but in the end turned out to have had nothing to do with the theft. Watching Jordan do his "interpretive seaweed" performance art (i.e. standing on stage very, very still while intense music played), Arthur was pleased to see Jordan was just as uniquely weird and wonderful as ever.

The next act was a Summerby entry. A girl hula-hooping. Arthur wanted to dismiss it,

but it was actually pretty
impressive. At one point,
she had five hula-hoops on
the go! Two on her arms,
two on her legs and one
around her middle. After
her, there was a country

singer, a rhythmic gymnast, a juggler ... even
a dancing dog! They'd seen so many talents, but
so far nothing to arouse suspicion.

"Grace," Arthur whispered. "I don't know
about you, but I'm starting to think nothing's
going to happen. What if we were wrong?"

"Same," Grace whispered back. "Maybe
the mole only wants to win sports games and
bake offs?"

"Maybe there is no mole after all," Arthur
concluded under his breath.

"Oh well, let's just enjoy the show," Grace
said. She couldn't hide that she was perturbed,

though. She wasn't used to her theories being wrong.

During the interval Grace, Arthur and Kieran – and Anna and Michael – went to interview the acts. It was even more annoying having to compete with Anna and Michael for interviews than it was having to compete with each other! Grace's hands curled into fists when Michael pipped her to the post for a chat with Bendy Boy. It felt like every time she saw a free contestant, he was in there first! She'd rather be beaten by Arthur – and that was saying something.

"Good luck beating Summerby," Michael said to her as they re-entered the hall for the second half.

Grace wrinkled her nose. "I think we'll be safe from your hula hoops." She sounded unfazed but she didn't actually mean it – the girl with the hula-hoops was pretty cool.

"Just wait until you see our dance troupe," Michael retorted.

Grace smiled. If Michael thought the Summerby dance group was good, they'd have nothing on the Victory Road team. She'd seen their routine when she interviewed them last week for a teaser on *Best of the Best*, and it was A-C-E. It even included a human pyramid.

The second half had some pretty great acts, but everyone was really waiting for the dance troupes to come on. Every year the show finished on the big, flashy numbers, and everyone knew they were saving the best until last.

Finally, there was a blackout and they heard four students get into position in the dark. It was time. The music blared so loudly you could feel it through your shoes and in your stomach. The air was thick with suspense.

"And now, we welcome the penultimate act

of the evening," Ms Lyall's voice boomed across the stage. "Please welcome to the stage *Strictly Summerby*!"

Lights came up on three Summerby girls and one boy. Grace recognized one of the girls as Tilly-Mae. *This is going to be interesting ...* she thought.

She looked across at Arthur in the dark. He was already looking at her, so clearly they were both thinking the same thing. If anything was about to go down, it was now. Was the Summerby team's routine going to go super well, only for Victory Road's to fall inexplicably flat on its face? They weren't sure what to expect.

The Summerby troupe did three short, sharp moves with their arms in unison. Then they started leaping across the stage, cutting across each other in diagonal motions. The crowds oohed and ahhed in delight, but Grace

frowned. This dance was awfully familiar . . .

When the four dancers started to build a human pyramid, Grace's hesitation turned to pure, gut-churning realization. Her stomach nosedived towards the floor. She'd expected foul play, but this was worse than she anticipated.

This was Victory Road's routine.

CHAPTER FIVE

[INTRO: *Anna's Amusings* jingle (7 secs).]

ANNA: And after a *stunning* dance performance by *Strictly Summerby*, Victory Road's dance troupe — *Victory Vibes* — are about to counter. Everyone is on the edge of their seats, waiting for the final and most anticipated act of the night. So far we've had bendy boys, dancing dogs, hurling hula-hoops ... What was your favourite act? Mine was Yodelling Yara. You can't beat a good yodel, in my opinion! Oh, and the moment's arrived ... *Victory Vibes* take to the stage. Will they be able to outdo the amazing *Strictly Summerby*? With three, short, sharp arm movements, they begin ... Oh ...

Gasps *Dying applause* *Whispers*

ANNA: Well this is awkward ...

As Victory Vibes danced on, Grace's heart was thudding. Waiting in the green room, they hadn't seen Summerby's performance, so they had no idea they were doing the *exact same routine*. She had to warn them somehow!

"Grace … Grace!" Arthur hissed. "We have to stop this!"

"I know …" Grace agreed, but she couldn't think of anything to do.

"Shall I … cause a scene? Run across the stage in my pants?" Arthur looked ready to, as well. *Bless him*, thought Grace. But not to mention the amount of trouble they'd get in, it was too late. The human pyramid was already under construction!

The routine was set to a different song so it took the audience a few moments to cotton on that it was the exact same dance they'd just watched Summerby do. But dawning realization had spread slowly across the sea of faces, including Ms Lyall.

All the teachers had looked at each other, muttering. Ms Lyall went a deep shade of puce and coughed like she'd just eaten a very spicy chilli. It seemed that no one, not even Ms Lyall, knew what to do. The performers, Lia included, could tell something was wrong too. They continued dancing with puzzled expressions.

Is Lia's confusion just a facade? wondered Grace. She seemed awfully convincing. But then what were she and Tilly-Mae whispering about right before their match? Had they been trading information about the dances?

Eventually, the routine ended and there was a slow smattering of applause. It was so quiet you could hear a man at the back of the balcony sneeze quietly.

Then the whispers started. "Copying ..." "Cheating ..." "Spied on Summerby ..."

Grace boiled with rage. Not only were the Victory Road dancers humiliated, but because they'd gone on last, it looked like *they* were the ones who copied Summerby! Grace couldn't *believe* that Summerby had done it again – and got away with it, right under their noses!

Ms Lyall took the stage. "Eh, *thank you*, girls," she said through gritted teeth to the baffled group. "And thank you everyone for coming to the tenth *Greenfair's Got Talent*. Please be assured, we will be looking into this ... ahem ... *mishap* immediately, and we will get to the bottom of it. Girls, a word in the green room, if you please."

Everyone was still muttering amongst themselves. Surely this was the point in the evening when a winner would be announced? Mr Pathak, Grace and Arthur's English teacher and their favourite of all the staff, rushed to the front to confer with Ms Lyall. The Summerby head teacher joined in and after some wild gesticulation between the heads, in which Mr

Pathak looked as if he was refereeing a tense conflict, Ms Lyall returned briefly to the stage.

"Given the, ahem ... circumstances ... we have decided that it is not appropriate for a winner to be declared this evening. Apologies to all and well done to *most* of tonight's performers."

There were disappointed cries of "What?!", "That's so unfair!" and "Cheaters ruin it for everyone!" The girls in the Victory Road dance group began filing off stage with Ms Lyall followed closely behind them. Grace knew they were in such big trouble. She studied Lia's face. Sure, she *looked* alarmed and upset, but that didn't prove her innocence. If she was behind this, of course she'd be hamming it up right now.

Before the exits could get clogged with audience members, Grace and Arthur were out of their seats.

"Kieran, could you stay here and watch our other suspects in case anything suspicious happens?" called Arthur. Grace's eyes travelled to Michael, already jumping out of his seat to find interviewees, and Diaz who had already approached him. Kieran nodded, and Arthur and Grace went off to investigate Lia and Tilly-Mae.

Thankfully, being school press, no one questioned Arthur and Grace's presence in the green room. A couple of the performers went bright red when they saw them, including the violinist that Anna was already interviewing, obviously hopeful for their chance to be on *Best of the Best* or *Radio Royalty*. Annoyingly, though, the members of the dance teams were nowhere to be seen.

"So, what do you think about everything that's gone down this evening?" Anna was asking.

"Most unfortunate," the girl said. "I imagine

the students involved won't want to show their faces on Monday."

"Yes, they should have been *moonwalking* on air, and now they're in quite the *twist* . . ." Anna went on.

Arthur was watching Anna's interview with a silly grin on his face. "Come on," Grace tugged his sleeve. "Now's not the time."

"But she's so good at puns . . ." Arthur said as Grace pulled him along.

Grace felt a flash of frustration at Arthur's inability to resist pun-based humour when there was an important task at hand.

The pair headed towards a private room just off the backstage area, which was no doubt where Ms Lyall had taken the Victory Road dance group. They lingered outside and could just hear snatches of Ms Lyall's voice, including phrases like "school's reputation", "serious matter" and "parents involved". Grace cringed.

71

Eventually the door opened. "Look nonchalant," Grace advised Arthur.

Arthur nodded, but wasn't convinced he knew what "nonchalant" meant.

Ms Lyall strode past them. She was probably off to have some grave conversations with parents. Then the four dancers, including Lia, trudged out looking miserable. Arthur and Grace stayed back and watched them from a distance. Tilly-Mae rushed over to Lia and gave her a hug. Arthur and Grace assessed them closely.

The interaction was quick. It seemed like just a conciliatory hug and nothing more. "Is that it?" Grace asked. She had felt sure she'd see a guilty look or a hushed whisper. Some sort of evidence. How could they have come away from this evening with nothing except another humiliating loss for Victory Road?

"I guess . . ." Arthur shrugged. "Maybe we were wrong. Maybe it's got nothing to do with them."

Grace shook her head, still sure of her theory. "They're not exactly going to congratulate each other about their plot in public, are they? Let's interview them. Maybe they'll accidentally give something away."

But before they could, Lia's parents marched into the room. They looked angry. Obviously Ms Lyall had caught up with them. They ushered their daughter over and indicated the door. Clearly, Lia was being taken home early.

No after-show celebrations for her.

As Lia followed her mum and dad, Grace felt their last hope slipping through their fingers. How were they supposed to investigate now?

But just as she felt herself deflate, Arthur tapped her frantically on the shoulder. "Grace, look!" He said, pointing at Tilly-Mae.

Grace turned to see Tilly-Mae darting out of the door behind Lia and her parents. Grace grinned. This was why she loved working as a team. If she'd been on her own, she'd have felt so downbeat about losing an interview with Lia that she would have missed Tilly-Mae's sudden departure.

Arthur and Grace followed immediately. Lia and her parents were up ahead, marching towards the exit, and Tilly-Mae was pacing quietly behind them at a distance. Grace's heart thudded. If this wasn't suspicious behaviour, then what was?

They followed Tilly-Mae, who was following Lia, all the way to the car park. Lia's parents went on ahead to their car, and Lia lingered behind, as if waiting for Tilly-Mae. Grace was impressed by how sleuthy Lia had been. She obviously knew Tilly-Mae was behind them, but she hadn't shown it, and her parents were none the wiser.

Then as Lia passed the school gate, Tilly-Mae ran up to her and Lia passed her an envelope. Blink and you'd have missed it. Lia didn't even look at Tilly-Mae, just carried on walking to the car, while Tilly-Mae began running back up to the school.

"Come on, Grace," Arthur said. "Let's get back inside before Tilly-Mae sees us."

Grace nodded, her mind racing. She *knew* they'd been on the right track. But just what was inside that envelope?

CHAPTER SIX

INTRO: *Best of the Best* jingle (7 secs)

INTRO: *Best of the Best* jingle (7 secs)

GRACE: Today on *Best of the Best's* Tech Troubles, we're joined by Mrs Romford, Victory Road librarian, who will be taking us through how to recover lost homework using the printer. You've been the school librarian for *forty-five years*, is that right Mrs Romford?

MRS ROMFORD: Ooooh yes. And I've seen *a lot* of lost homework in my time, believe you me. Why, I remember one poor lass ... She left her French A-Level coursework on a bus and her computer died. All that work, gone! Kaput! It seemed like all was lost, until *I* helped her access the printing records ...

It was the day after the talent show and the trio had headed to the library, with Arthur garbling a story about having "printed-my-homework-but-lost-it-then-deleting-the-file". Sure, sweet, kindly Mrs Romford definitely knew her way around the computer, which was somewhat surprising for a woman in her seventies, but, wow, she was very ... very ... slow ...

Grace couldn't help tapping her foot as Mrs Romford typed one ... finger ... at ... a ... time. How could a woman know how to access printing records but not type with two hands?

"Here we are," she said, what felt like years later. Grace dived forward. On screen, Grace, Arthur and Kieran could see a list of what every student at Victory Road had printed the day before! "Now, what was it you said you were looking for, young man?" Mrs Romford peered at Arthur over her spectacles.

Thankfully, at that moment there was the sound of a glass knocking over. "No liquids near the books!" Mrs Romford shrieked as she shuffled away.

"Quick!" Grace hissed.

All they needed to do was search Lia's name and *voila!* They hurriedly printed off the document and stared at each other open mouthed. They weren't sure what they were expecting, but it wasn't ...

... a *school transfer form*.

"What does it mean?" Kieran breathed.

"Lia is obviously leaving to join Summerby Secondary," Grace whispered back.

"But why would she give this to Tilly-Mae?" Kieran asked.

"*Look*." Arthur pointed. "There's a section for references from a student who attends your chosen school."

The truth was blindingly obvious. Arthur

shook his head. He still couldn't believe Lia, the positive, smiley, friendly girl they all knew and loved, was transferring to Summerby and leaking all their secrets. Leaving the school was one thing – but actively *betraying* them? He couldn't wrap his head around it.

"I don't *believe*—" Grace started to yell, but lots of angry eyes swivelled from their books in her direction. One girl put her finger to her lips. ". . . it!" Grace finished in a whisper. "We've got to go and confront them, now!"

Kieran put his hand on Grace's arm. "Woah, woah, remember Roddy and Bea?"

Grace paused for a beat and nodded. They all remembered the time they'd accused the pair of stealing the chess trophy and been breathtakingly wrong.

"The transfer form," Arthur explained, "is what's known as *circumstantial evidence*. Circumstantial evidence is . . ."

"I know what circumstantial evidence is, thanks, Arthur," Grace tutted.

Arthur pretended not to be disappointed. He'd thought he had something to teach Grace for once, and was looking forward to telling her all about how circumstantial evidence could point you in a certain direction, whereas proof was undeniable.

"Well," he continued. "Given that we've broken our promise not to interfere in official school matters again, we're going to need something more to give Ms Lyall. What we need is *proof*."

Grace didn't argue. Arthur guessed she was also remembering how much trouble they'd got in the last time. Sometimes Arthur still had nightmares about his microphone (Mikey) being taken away from him by a furious Ms Lyall. This time, they needed to be absolutely sure.

"We need to act fast, though," Grace added.

"The last Summerby versus Victory Road league match of the season is *this afternoon*. And you can bet Tilly-Mae and Lia have something planned for it."

Arthur massaged his temples. "I think I know how we can do this."

"What are you thinking?" Kieran asked.

"I'm thinking ... we're going to need Misha's help."

***

Kieran put his hands on Misha's shoulders. "Are you ready, Misha?"

It was another sunny day at Greenfair, and everyone at Victory Road was pumped to try and win back their dignity, especially as it was their last game against Summerby in the league.

Misha nodded. She looked nervous, though. They'd agreed that the only way they could gain proof of Lia and Tilly-Mae's conspiracy was to feed false information to them. If they responded to the false information, and no one else knew about it (this was key), it would prove without a doubt that they were guilty. "I feel so guilty, though, turning up when I told Lia I was injured ..."

Misha was always centre forward. She was amazingly fast and brilliant at getting the ball in the net, so it made sense. There was one girl – Jen Barnaby – who without exception marked Misha at every game, because she was the fastest on the Summerby team. Whenever Misha wasn't playing, they didn't use Jen, to make sure she was rested and on top form for games against Misha. If Misha divulged this information to Lia and Lia only, and Jen didn't show, then they would know that Lia was the leak.

What Victory Road were really going to

do was play more attacking players today than usual and have less focus on defence. It was win-win, thought Arthur. They were going to catch out Lia and, using their real secret tactics, they were also going to beat Summerby for the first time in months!

"OK, call Kieran," Grace instructed.

Misha called Kieran from her phone, and hit record. If they got Lia red-handed on tape, they'd have solid recorded evidence to take to Ms Lyall.

Grace jerked her head toward the changing area. "Let's go, Misha."

"Godspeed," Kieran and Arthur said at the same time, and did their classic Radio Royalty bow to Misha. Grace smirked. Only Kieran and Arthur could joke around at a time like this.

Misha followed Grace toward the locker rooms looking nervous, but determined. When they had explained the situation to her she had been ready to do anything to protect her team. Her bravery had warmed their hearts. If anyone caught her she would be in serious trouble.

As they walked, Grace looked around at Greenfair. It was beautiful. Especially as spring had just sprung. She couldn't believe anyone would want to destroy this to build luxury flats. Where would they all go to play football, or just to hang out in the sunshine, or for a winter walk? Grace looked up through the branches of the giant tree they'd been sitting under and remembered hiding behind it before throwing a giant snowball at her two brothers when she was just six years old. The day before, they'd showered her with snow, soaking her through. She'd vowed to get them back, and this tree had helped her do it. She had memories in every corner of this place. She thought nervously of the protests, and the big contest to broadcast them to the nation. She so wanted to help the protesters' message reach as many people as possible.

Right now, though, there was another important matter to attend to. When they reached the locker rooms they split up, Misha putting her bag next to Lia's. Grace gave her one last reassuring nod.

Arthur and Kieran, meanwhile, listened intently to the conversation at the other end of the phone.

They heard Misha's voice. "Oh, Lia, hi."

"Misha?" Lia exclaimed. "What are you doing here? I thought you said you weren't playing today? Is your foot OK?"

"OH!" Misha replied. "Yes, mysterious recovery. Miracle cure. Aloe vera and, erm… banana skin."

Kieran hung up. "She's good. All right, let's roll."

The pair went outside and sat underneath the shade of a giant oak tree at the edge of the park. The players were lining up the field. Arthur and Kieran moved closer to the pitch. This was the moment of truth.

The Summerby team all took position. Arthur and Kieran watched as Jen Barnaby jogged onto the field. Kieran and Arthur shook their heads and exchanged a disappointed glance with Misha. They were wrong ... There was no way Lia was the leak! If she'd told Summerby that Misha wasn't playing today, Jen definitely wouldn't be playing either!

What happened next was worse. Jen joined the back line of defence where they had extra players. Almost like they knew Summerby were planning on relaxing their defences today in order to focus on scoring.

"What ... How did ..." Arthur spluttered.

Summerby knew. They knew! They had

Victory Road's real tactics yet again – their decoy had done nothing! Arthur couldn't believe it. He looked over at Grace, whose blood was clearly boiling. She hated being outsmarted. Jen stood in defence with a smug smirk on her face.

Arthur put his head in his hands. "Nooo, it wasn't Lia! She's not the mole."

"But ... but ..." Kieran was lost for words. "But she's transferring to Summerby! How could it not be her?" he finished.

They looked between Lia and Tilly-Mae. Tilly-Mae was waving at Lia, whose face lit up as she greeted her friend.

"Unless ..." Arthur started.

"Unless?" Kieran questioned.

Arthur had a look on his face like he was figuring out some really complicated long division. "Did the transfer form have a name on it?" he asked, looking between Lia and Tilly-

Mae. "Could it be...?"

Kieran suddenly clocked his meaning, but it was too late now. The whistle blew and the game was about to start.

Anna's voice floated over from a nearby tree. "Is that ... Misha Klimach in defence I see? Are they experimenting with probability theory, perhaps?"

They could also hear Michael recording notes for his next Summerby Stories piece into his Dictaphone. "And, in a somewhat bizarre, baffling and, quite frankly, probably disastrous move, Victory Road have decided to play their star striker as a left-back. This is going to be interesting ..."

"Come on," Arthur said. "Forget the mole…We could still win! Let's rally! Maybe if we cheer really hard for Victory Road, it will boost their morale.'

But ten minutes later, they were already two-nil down. Misha and Grace's energy had sunk. Arthur and Kieran were slumped defeatedly on the grass, whereas Anna and Michael were leaping around as the Summerby team scored. They had to admit it – it was hopeless. Victory Road were facing yet another loss and not only that, their radio shows were going to bomb yet again as a result.

At half time they were three-nil down, and the Victory Road players trudged gloomily off the field. Grace sat down next to Arthur and Kieran wordlessly. The Summerby players, however, bustled with an irritating amount of buzz and chatter. You could almost feel the excitable energy radiating off them in waves. Only one player hadn't joined in the celebration: Tilly-Mae.

"Hey, chin up, I'll be on the team next term and then maybe we'll win," she called out. "I shouldn't be saying this, but my transfer just got approved and I'm like a kangaroo on a pogo stick. Can't wait to join Victory Road, guys. Honestly. It's a great school and if you're all as nice as Lia, I'll be like a pig in mud."

"Eh?" said Arthur.

"I can't translate as well as Lia, but I think she means she's excited," Grace whispered behind her hand.

So it was true: Tilly-Mae was the one transferring, not Lia. Kieran, Arthur and Grace looked at each other. How wrong could they have been?

Grace feigned surprise. "Oh, that's ... unexpected, Tilly-Mae! We can't wait to have you." She smiled weakly. She was genuinely pleased that Tilly-Mae was joining their school, but they'd been so off-base in their calculations! And now they were going to lose again as a result.

Tilly-Mae jogged off to catch up with the Summerby team, and the three stared after her.

"I guess that's that, then," Kieran concluded. "It definitely wasn't Lia and Tilly-Mae."

Arthur blew air through his lips in frustration and Grace took an exasperated bite of her half-time puff puffs.

"Yep, back to square one."

"We'll get them," said Arthur. "Not today. But we will."

Just then, Grace's phone beeped. She looked down and read her notification in horror. "Guys, have you seen …?"

They all stared down at Grace's phone in shock. Just when they thought this day couldn't get any worse …

CHAPTER SEVEN

[INTRO: Breaking news music (3 secs).]

ANNA: BREAKING NEWS! This just in: *Anna's Amusings* can EXCLUSIVELY reveal that new evidence has been found relating to what people have been calling the "Double Dance Disaster". Sources have revealed that both teams had outsourced their routines to the SAME choreographer ...

Arthur sighed. As if it wasn't bad enough that he, Kieran and Grace had wasted time pursuing the wrong lead, in doing so they'd missed the *real* scoop of the week. There was no point doing a segment about it now.

Nearly all of Victory Road had obviously already listened to Anna's breaking news bulletin online.

"Guys, this is a disaster," Kieran said. "We're nowhere in the investigation and our ratings are lower than *ever.*"

It was the day after the last Summerby versus Victory Road girls' match of the season, and Grace was slumped forward with her head in her hands. She hated losing to Summerby's radio shows even more than she hated losing to their football team. "All that time we spent investigating Tilly-Mae and Lia, and they'd just booked the same choreographer?!" she scowled.

"I guess," Arthur shrugged.

"No!" Grace sat up. She had a wild look in her eye. "No, it doesn't make any sense! What about all the other losses? What, are we supposed to buy that they were all just big coincidences?"

Arthur and Kieran shook their heads. They didn't think these were coincidences any more than Grace did.

Anna's voice carried on playing in the background. "How unfortunate for everyone involved ..."

"Yes, but more unfortunate for Victory Road, wasn't it?" Grace yelled.

"Woah, Grace, it's not Anna's fault," defended Arthur.

"Isn't it?" Grace raised one eyebrow. "Now we've totally ruled out Tilly-Mae, who are the only two people left with something to gain from winning every single school event, eh? Answer me that, Arthur!"

Arthur's heart sank. Anna and Michael. He had been thinking the same thing.

"Look, it's not Anna, OK." Arthur's heart was beating faster. It *couldn't* be Anna. She was funny and nice and ... and smelled of coconut mixed with limes! Plus, if it *was* her, then he couldn't help that sneaking guilty feeling that he'd given away information to her. If that were true, then he would have accidentally *helped* her bring down Victory Road. "It *has* to be Michael," he asserted. "And his accomplice, Diaz."

Grace sighed. Anyone could see that Arthur was letting his heart get in the way of his head.

"Anna was the one who broke this scoop, not Michael," she concluded.

Kieran pulled a *yikes* face at Arthur. "Mate, Grace is right . . . What do we *really* know about—"

"Look, I trust Anna," Arthur repeated. "You've been determined that it's her from the beginning, even before she broke that scoop." He turned to Grace. "Why are you so fixated on her? What, are you jealous?"

As soon as he'd said it, Arthur regretted it. He didn't mean it, he was just desperate for it not to be Anna.

Grace opened her mouth to counter, but closed it again. She felt hurt by Arthur's words, but she couldn't deny ... She *was* a bit jealous. Not that she'd ever admit that out loud.

"OK, fine," Grace agreed quietly, ignoring Arthur's comment. "We'll rule out Anna."

Grace still had her suspicions, and there was also something she hadn't told Arthur: while he and Anna were talking, she had seen her scribbling in a little, red notebook when he wasn't looking. But she couldn't say that now without sounding petty.

Kieran stared at his shoes and whistled awkwardly.

"OK, so we start with Diaz," Arthur said, trying to shake the tension from the air.

"Yup, Diaz," Grace repeated.

"It *is* weird that Diaz had started showing up at all sorts of events with his buddy Michael, just as soon as Victory Road started losing everything," Kieran added.

Grace cleared her throat. "We should go to something Diaz has always been a part of. Something from before he became a fan of girls' football and dance and everything else he's been attending."

Arthur followed her train of thought. "The debate club!"

"Excellent!" Kieran clapped his hands with false brightness. "They meet at lunchtime, don't they? In the east wing? We can probably still join in if we hurry. Let's go!"

He leapt out the door. Grace and Arthur followed behind. Neither of them really wanted to be around the other right now, but they needed to work together.

On the way over they worked out their plan: they would pretend they were there for a general piece on the debate team, and try to find out anything they could.

When they arrived, a heated political discussion was already in place. Mr Pathak, who ran the club, welcomed them in but held his finger to his lips. Two students stood, each with a podium in front of them, and they were surprised to see that one of them was Roddy Lyall, the headmistress's son. Shy Roddy had covered up for his little brother, Benjy, who had stolen the chess trophy (from Misha Klimach, the original thief) last term. They would *never* have expected to see Roddy in front of so many people, arguing until he was blue in the face!

"Looks like Misha's not the only one to have come out of her shell," Grace whispered.

"An undeniably good point," Roddy said to his opponent, a stern-looking older girl. "But if you look at it *this* way . . ."

"GO, *RODDY*!" Kieran said under his breath. "He's really found his voice."

When the debate was over, Roddy and his opponent sat down. The rest of the debate team noticed Grace, Arthur and Kieran's appearance and began whispering amongst each other. Even though ratings were down, everyone still wanted to appear on their shows.

Sitting up front was Diaz, who waved at them and smiled warmly. For a fleeting second, Arthur thought, *Maybe he is just a really supportive kid who goes along to random events for no reason at all.* His smile was convincing, that was for sure. But then Arthur snapped out of it. If Diaz wasn't feeding Michael information, then he'd have to consider Anna as a suspect.

They set up their equipment ready for interviews.

"OK ... here we go." Arthur nodded towards Diaz. This was their real chance to find out something useful – straight from the horse's mouth.

Tentatively, they approached Diaz together. He was handing out schedules for the next meeting.

"Diaz, as the team's co-founder, we wanted your insight before anyone else's ..." Grace opened.

Diaz seemed to believe that they were genuine. "Sure."

"So, you meet twice a week on Tuesdays and Thursdays, right?" said Kieran, holding the mic out to Diaz.

"Yes, five minutes after last bell. We have one subject per week, each student will get the chance to argue for and against. We do five mini-debates per session, each one five minutes long with five-minute breaks."

"That's quite a strict schedule to keep ... Do the debates ever overrun?" Arthur asked.

Diaz tapped his wrist. "Not on my watch!" He was obviously a stickler.

101

"We saw the *Summerby Stories* piece on making the international championships. Amazing!" Grace complimented, slyly moving the conversation over to Michael.

"Thanks." Diaz smiled.

"Michael Bernard from Summerby is your best mate, right? How long have you known him?" Arthur continued.

"We used to live on the same street. That was before Michael moved in with his mum and changed his name and stuff . . ."

They continued probing, but it was hard to find out much about their friendship without making it *too* obvious, and Diaz kept bringing the conversation back to the team. Unsurprisingly, being a top debater meant he was well-practiced at keeping to the point.

"Well, thanks for talking to us, Diaz," Grace said flatly as the interview drew to a close. They had to move on to other students before their interest in Diaz became noticeable.

"No problem!" Diaz replied, and he went over to tell a pair of debaters their time was up.

It was frustrating they hadn't managed to get anything out of him, but they felt hopeful the other students might share something useful. They weren't exactly a shy and retiring bunch. However, with such a chatty group, it became increasingly difficult to keep steering the conversation back to Diaz.

"So who are the longest running members of the debate team?" Arthur asked one girl.

"Um, me, and Jodie, and Diaz. We started the club."

"Great, and you're all still involved? No one's taking a back seat whilst they, say, pursue other activities?" asked Arthur, hinting at Diaz's sudden interest in sports.

"Erm, well Jodie recently took up crochet . . . She made me this *stunning* egg cosy . . ."

Not the answer Arthur was looking for.

By the end of three interviews, Arthur had gained nothing except that Diaz was reliable and kept things running super smoothly. He was also the proud new owner of one of Jodie's crocheted egg cosies. He hoped Grace and Kieran had done better, but as soon as he saw their faces, he knew they hadn't.

"All everyone has to say about Diaz is that he's super organized," Kieran shrugged.

"Yeah, he makes sure everyone's here on the dot for every meeting, has never missed a single week since the club started, blah, blah ..." Grace sighed. "Ugh! We have nada! Zilch!"

They began packing up silently, feeling dejected, when Roddy approached them. "Hey, guys."

"Roddy, my man!" Kieran fist-bumped him and Roddy looked pleased.

"You were ace up there," Arthur said.

"Thanks." Roddy grinned.

"So how's life as a big debate star?" Grace asked. She was disappointed they hadn't found anything, but it was nice to see Roddy.

"This isn't another secret grilling, is it?" Roddy asked cautiously.

Grace laughed. "No, I was just asking, I swear."

Roddy raised one eyebrow jokingly. "Sorry I can't stay to talk, guys. I've got to move the podium for Diaz."

Grace, Arthur and Kieran looked at each other.

"For Diaz?" Grace tried to sound casual.

"Yeah, Diaz usually does it, but he leaves ten minutes early on Thursdays."

"Since when?" asked Arthur, barely containing his excitement.

"Hmm . . . a couple of months ago, I guess?"

Roddy said his goodbyes, looking slightly confused by their sudden, enthusiastic questions about Diaz's schedule. Once he was out of earshot, Arthur whispered, "Yesssss!" and Kieran punched the air.

"Leave early?" Grace hissed. "The boy who never misses a meeting? No ... that doesn't fit at all!"

As Grace was always saying about her crime novels, ninety per cent of the time it was something apparently insignificant that led the detective to solving the case. It wasn't much, but it *was* a clue. Diaz had changed his routine. The routine he had maintained so steadfastly for two whole years. There *must* be a reason.

CHAPTER EIGHT

[Wildlife music, whispering ...]

ARTHUR: And the unwavering Diaz glides smoothly through the hallway ... saying hello to every passing teacher ... waving at every rogue student ... as he does every single day ...

KIERAN: Aaand in a characteristic display of reliability he arrives early yet again ... To sit in the same chair ... As he does in every lesson ...

Arthur switched Mikey off. "I'm losing my mind," he declared.

"Me too." Even Kieran looked weary. And it was really hard to make Kieran look that way – he was almost permanently cheery and enthusiastic.

"A whole week!" Arthur cried. "A whole week of *this*!"

"And he's not so much as gone for a spontaneous loo break," Kieran finished in disbelief. "Not *one*," said Arthur. "Who has that kind of bladder control?"

Kieran snorted. "I mean, speak for yourself."

"I told you, I spilled a glass of water that time, all right!" Arthur crossed his arms. The great water-trousers incident of Summer Camp 2018. He'd never lived it down.

Kieran raised his hands. "Sure, sure."

"All I meant was, I've never known another twelve-year-old to be so ... so ..." Arthur struggled for the right word. "Urgh, Grace would know what to say."

"Pedantic?" said a smug voice to their left. Grace had arrived to join them. Kieran waved.

"Yeah ..." Arthur agreed, although he didn't know what that meant.

"He *is* very good at time-keeping," Grace added. "You know, I've timed his walk from the Science block to the Art block every morning and it takes him *exactly* fifty-eight seconds every single time."

"No *way!*" Kieran seemed impressed.

"Every. Single. Time." Grace nodded.

The trio had spent the past week taking it in turns to watch Diaz, looking for any other breaks in his routine, or trying to overhear conversations with Michael. They'd had no luck. The boy was like a robot. He even unpacked his books and pencils in the exact same way, and chose the same pudding every day. There was absolutely nothing to note. He was a model student, which also meant he was never on his phone talking to Michael, so there was nothing to draw from that either.

"What's worse, he seems to be friendly with *everyone*," Kieran commented. "He doesn't seem like the kind of boy to go grassing up all these different teams."

"Ah, I reached a different conclusion on that," Grace said. "I think that because Diaz is friendly with everyone, it makes him *more* likely to be our culprit. He's sort-of friends with everyone but also sort-of friends with no one. Michael seems like his only true friend. Plus he must have access to *all sorts* of information."

Arthur raised his eyebrows. He hadn't thought of it that way, but it was good to hear Grace's perspective. They had been talking so much less since things had become weird between them. He didn't like it, but he didn't know how to change it.

"Either way, it's nearly time," Kieran added. "Our last chance to have *anything* to show for this week."

Grace nodded. It was Thursday, the day of Diaz's supposed routine change. They were going to wait outside the debate room as the club met for after-school practice, and hope that he left ten minutes early as Roddy had described. If he did, they'd be there to follow him. Grace felt sure they hadn't wasted their time tracking Diaz. Even though she'd suspected Anna initially – and still did – over the week she'd become sure that Diaz had something to hide. He was *too* perfect. Anyone who lived their life with that level of precision was surely keeping a well-concealed secret. Plus, knowing he was *quite* so precise, his sudden change in routine seemed even more suspicious.

If he wasn't hiding anything ... Well, it would be another dead end. And Grace wouldn't dare bring up Anna again as a possibility. Her heart sank a little as she thought of how off things had been between her and Arthur.

But there was no time for that now. The debate club was starting to arrive.

Grace, Arthur and Kieran had identified a classroom opposite that remained empty during the debate club's Thursday practice. The room had a good view out of the window that overlooked the path leading towards the school gates, so when Diaz left, they would spot him. For the meantime, they hid under a table in case someone happened to come in.

So there was nothing to do but wait.

Across the hallway, they heard Mr Pathak handing out "for" and "against" cards. Usually they would be joking around and having fun right now, even if they were in the middle of a serious investigation, but the atmosphere between Grace and Arthur was stiff. Kieran rapped his fingernails on the leg of the table. It was going to be a long afternoon.

They sat there in the same way for thirty minutes, making some small talk at first, mostly started by Kieran, but that quickly faded out. Every so often Arthur would glance at his phone, sure he'd killed ten minutes, only to realize that just a minute had passed. Still, this was journalism. It wasn't all glamour and exciting scoops.

Kieran pointed at his phone. "OK, eleven minutes left. Diaz should be leaving at any moment."

Arthur nodded, and moved to crawl out from under the table and head towards the window, when suddenly the door opened.

Arthur quickly retracted his arm. All three of them froze.

A pair of boots strode into the room. The person was talking on the phone and they instantly recognized the voice as Mr Pathak.

"No, I can't do that – could I book in for four p.m. instead?"

His shoes moved closer to the table that Grace, Arthur and Kieran were hiding beneath. His trouser leg brushed Kieran's arm. The three of them held their breath as tightly as possible. They all loved Mr P, but if he found them here their cover would be blown. They'd have to leave and the entire mission would be ruined. It might even get back to Ms Lyall and then she'd be watching them like a hawk ... especially after all the trouble they caused her last term.

Grace wracked her brains for excuses, but drew a blank. How could they possibly explain lurking beneath a table in an empty classroom after school? Meanwhile, Arthur was panicking that they were missing Diaz's exit. Mr P had walked in just at the moment he should be on the way to his secret meeting!

Eventually, Mr P left the room. Quick as a cat, Arthur bolted out from under the table towards the window. He was *just* in time to see Diaz's stripy scarf disappear out of the school gates and around the corner.

"He's gone," Arthur yelled. "Now!" He grabbed Grace and Kieran's arms, all awkwardness momentarily forgotten, and the three of them sprinted out of the classroom and out of the building.

But by the time they made it onto the street, Diaz had vanished. Arthur kicked the wall in frustration. They'd spent nearly an hour sitting under a table practically in silence for nothing!

"I can't *believe* I missed my mum's meatballs for this," said Kieran wistfully.

"Yes, *that's* the real loss here," Arthur replied through gritted teeth.

"Look," Grace said, ever practical. "It's fifty-fifty. Left or right. We choose the right way and we might still catch him."

Arthur closed his eyes and breathed in. "Left!" he yelled.

Without hesitation the three of them ran left, and as they reached the end of the road, they saw Diaz's colourful scarf up ahead. Grace put her hands in the air. Kieran fist-pumped and mouthed, "SCORE!"

They were back on Diaz's tail!

There was no time to lose. They moved quickly down the street, following him at speed, but making sure to maintain a reasonable distance. They tracked him all the way down the high street, past the shops and through some quiet residential streets, and it was only after two more minutes that Kieran whispered, "Guys. I have a feeling . . ."

They *all* had a feeling. They'd been here before, for school events. And as the Summerby Secondary sign loomed up ahead, all of their suspicions about Diaz seemed to be confirmed.

CHAPTER NINE

SUMMERBY *STORIES*

NEWS : SPORTS : ENTERTAINMENT : INTERVIEWS AND MORE

SUMMERBY COSTUME CUPBOARD GIVEAWAY!

By Michael Bernard

Due to the "unmanageable" amount of clothes that have been accumulated by Summerby's top-rated drama department, Head of Drama, Mr Sanford, has taken the decision to downscale its collection by a third. "We're very grateful for the generosity of students and parents over the years, but we need to make room for new costumes," he commented.

From this week onwards, a number of unwanted items are up for grabs. From vintage jackets and designer shoes, to elegant hats and fascinators, to classic gowns ... **<u>everything must go.</u>**

The notice in *Summerby Stories* had been right: the cupboard really did have everything! They were sure to find the perfect disguise to go undercover and spy on Diaz.

It was possible, Grace thought as she took off her fire-woman's hat, that they may have got a *little* distracted ...

Arthur had a pillow stuffed under his Tudor gear, and he held up a decapitated doll head. "Guys, guys, who am I?"

"Henry the eighth, obviously. At least give us a challenge," Grace snorted.

Kieran, who was sporting alien antennae and holding a baby Jesus, looked confused. "Who?" he mouthed at Arthur.

Suddenly Grace spotted the time. It was nearly half past four. "OK, OK, enough of this. We'll miss Diaz! First things first. Who's infiltrating?"

Grace and Kieran's heads swung towards Arthur.

"Why are you looking at *me*?!" he cried.

"Because you're good at this sort of thing, mate," Kieran said.

"What exactly is *this sort of thing*?" Every muscle in Arthur's body was tightening.

"Look at it this way. Grace is a Ravenclaw, brainy and good at plans and stuff. You're a Gryffindor, brave and ready to leap into danger," Kieran explained.

"And what about you? Aren't you a Gryffindor?" Arthur wasn't going to let Kieran wriggle out of this.

"I'm a Hufflepuff," Kieran said, as if it was obvious. "Good at moral support."

"All right, *oh, Sorting Hat,*" Arthur spluttered. "What a convenient house you've put yourself in. Personally, I think we should flip for it."

Kieran shrugged and reached in his pocket for a coin. He threw it in the air.

"Heads!" Arthur called.

It was tails. They did it again with Grace, and once again Arthur called wrong.

"The coins have spoken, Arthur," Kieran declared.

Arthur's shoulders had sagged in defeat. Why was it always him sneaking into caretaker's huts and now going undercover in schools he didn't attend?

"Now *that's* settled ..." Grace sprang into

action-mode and began sifting through the piles of clothes with fresh determination. "What about this?" She pulled something out of a box that looked like a dead ginger guinea pig.

Arthur recoiled. "What *is* that?"

"A wig! You're going to need to change your hair." She stuck it on Arthur's head.

"And some glasses." Kieran leaned in and slotted some large, round-rimmed frames behind his ears.

It was difficult to find an outfit from a wardrobe meant for theatrical productions that didn't look totally bizarre, but in the end they settled on a lumpy brown jumper and corduroy trousers. Arthur inspected himself in a mirror.

"I'm a walking crime against fashion!" he cried in horror.

"Thankfully no one will recognize you," Grace comforted.

Kieran patted him on the shoulder. "Or so we hope."

"I thought you were supposed to be *good* at moral support?" Arthur retorted.

In a stroke of luck, Grace had remembered that there was a French exchange programme happening at Summerby at the moment. (She'd been speaking to some of the students to practise her grammar, obviously.) If Arthur pretended he was a French exchange student, no one would mind if he didn't say much. And the less he spoke, the less chance he had of giving himself away.

They'd dubbed him Pierre, which was Kieran's suggestion. Grace had protested that was too stereotypical, but after going round a few less conventional French names (such as Gabin and Rémy) they circled back around to Pierre as it was the only one Arthur could convincingly pronounce.

Kieran put both hands on Arthur's shoulders. "OK, are you ready, Arthur?"

"No," Arthur squeaked. What if he got caught? At least so far he'd only got into trouble at his own school. He dreaded to think how angry Ms Lyall would be if he embarrassed her by getting into trouble at *another school*.

"You'll be fine. You can do it! We believe in you, Pierre!" Grace added.

Arthur smiled. If there was one good thing about walking into the lion's den, it was that he and Grace were too preoccupied to be weird with one another.

"OK, I'm going in," Arthur croaked. He started to walk towards the classroom Diaz had entered, but turned to wave at Grace and Kieran one final time. Kieran saluted him solemnly.

Arthur felt like a dead man walking. Even though he was in disguise, it was like the hallways of his rival school *knew* he wasn't supposed to be there. Like the whole building was watching him. And what if he ran into someone he knew – like Anna? He gulped. Would his disguise be good enough?

Arthur tried to breathe and focus. He patted his phone, which was set to record, and went over Pierre's history again. What had they said? He was born in Normandy. Or was it Giverny? He couldn't remember anything Grace had said. He was staying with a girl called Bernadette? Argh! In the end, they'd only had *three minutes* to prepare. Why had he spent so much time pretending to be Henry the Eighth? His back story was patchy, but it would have to do. Hopefully no one would ask him any questions anyway.

As Arthur approached the door, his heart was in his mouth. He turned the doorknob and entered. If this was some secret Victory Road takedown meeting, he was about to find out.

***

When he walked into the room, Arthur was half expecting to see a board with "DESTROY VICTORY ROAD" and "EVIL SCHEMES" written on it, but there was just a small group of students sitting in a circle holding notepads. Diaz had taken a seat at the far side of the room, next to Michael, and Arthur thanked his lucky stars there were no seats left near them. It would be easier to fly under the radar sitting next to someone he didn't know.

He was just about to sit down when someone tapped him on the shoulder. He turned and was surprised to see a much older student smiling down at him.

"Hi! We haven't seen you here before, right? I'm Esperanza, welcome!" She reached out her hand and Arthur shook it. She must run the club, he thought. So was she involved in the plot, too. But why would an older student be interested in whether a bunch of year seven and eight students won against Victory Road or not?

"Erm," He cleared his throat. Time to try out his dodgy French accent. "I'm . . . Pieeerre."

"Oh, great, nice to meet you, Pierre! On the exchange programme, right?"

Arthur nodded. Thankfully, Esperanza didn't ask "Pierre" any more questions. She gestured to a clipboard in the corner. "The sign-up sheet is over there."

Arthur was so nervous he took one step forward and fumbled over his feet. Quick as a flash, Esperanza put her arm out to catch him.

"You're lucky my mother's a dance teacher," she said.

Arthur smiled briefly and headed over, carefully, and wrote his name down on the sheet. That couldn't happen again. He didn't want to attract any more unwanted attention.

He'd hoped the sign-up sheet might give him a clue about this meeting, but it was literally just a list of names so he still had no idea what he was signing up *for*. *Pierre* . . . he scribbled. Rubbish! They hadn't come up with a last name! What were some French last names? He settled on "Pierre McFrance" and hurried away.

Finally getting to a seat, Arthur was out of the danger zone. But not for long. Someone small and glossy and smelling of coconut mixed with lime sat down next to him and Arthur's eyes shifted to one side while every muscle clenched.

It was Anna.

She looked directly at him. "Hi. Are you new here?"

Why did she have to be so nice and friendly – why couldn't she just have ignored him? Arthur obviously couldn't reply – his French accent was terrible, and what if she recognized his voice?

He was filled with conflicted feelings ... The fact that she was so welcoming to a slightly oddball, badly dressed kid with a mop that looked like a dead guinea pig made him like her even more. But why was she here? Was she in on it too? Suddenly, Arthur found himself praying this was all a big mix-up.

"This is Pierre," Esperanza cut in before Arthur had a chance to reply.

"Hi, Pierre." Anna smiled. *That smile. That smell.* Anna couldn't be involved, could she?

Before she could keep chatting to him, Esperanza clapped her hands together. "We're already running late, so I'd love to get started ASAP. Right, guys, welcome to the third meeting of FemSoc!"

Femme Sock? Was this about ... socks?

"Does anyone have anything to report back about last week's assignments?"

Anna raised her hand. "Diaz was *amazing*.

He did such great work at the girls' football matches."

Everyone whooped and Diaz gave a shy smile. Arthur's heart dropped into his shoes. Great work? Like . . . great *spying* work?

"Well done, Diaz," Esperanza clasped her hands together. "As we all know, girls' sports are not only *ten times* less well-funded than boys' but they are less well-attended too. This is the excuse given *not* to fund girls' sports, but without the funding it's very difficult to achieve bigger audiences, so it's a vicious cycle. We need more supporters, and not just girls, but boys too . . ." She looked to Diaz. "To back our corner, show their appetite, to come out and say this is not OK. Now, a few other things on the Feminist Society agenda . . ."

Arthur's heart slowed way down. His clenched muscles relaxed. FemSoc = *Feminist Society*.

That was why Diaz had suddenly started

showing up to random football matches! He wasn't a mole ... He was a *feminist!*

Arthur could have burst out laughing. Not just because of Diaz – that was bad news, really, because if Diaz wasn't involved, they were back to square one – but, if this was just a feminist society meeting, then Anna was in the clear, too. For now.

He leaned back in his chair, feeling like a right lemon but also buzzing with relief. He was vindicated!

But the moment was short-lived.

As Arthur leaned back, he glimpsed the inside of Anna's notebook as she flicked through to find her page. Written down in large capital letters he saw some scribbled words that made his heart sink: "Arthur" and "tactics".

She'd taken notes about what he said before the Summerby versus Victory Road game!

Arthur tried to peer closer, but she'd already

passed over the page to a fresh sheet, and all he could do was sit there in stunned silence. Had Grace been right all along?

Maybe Anna couldn't be trusted . . .

CHAPTER TEN

> [Intro: Chart show jingle (3 secs).]
>
> **ARTHUR:** It's *Radio Royalty's* Most Played Tuuuunes Of The Week — these are the songs I've had on repeat this week … because, well … cough … anyway, in at number 3, we have … "Back to Black" by Amy Winehouse. I don't actually own any black clothes but I've been thinking about buying some, recently. *Cough* Ahem, moving on … In second place it's "Love Will Tear Us Apart" by Joy Division … I never really understood this song until … *Cough* Ahem, it doesn't matter …

Arthur was about to announce his number one choice when there was a soft knock at his door.

Arthur's dad poked his head into the room.

"You OK, son?" he asked.

"Um, fine," Arthur answered unconvincingly.

His dad pointed at the bed. "Mind if I sit?"

Arthur nodded.

His dad entered and paused Joy Division. "Great song," he commented. "I've played a lot of songs about heartbreak in my time."

Arthur's dad was in a band, *Lad Dadz,* i.e. the most embarrassing band on the planet.

"Heartbreak? What? I'm not playing songs about *heartbreak*," Arthur spluttered. "These just happen to be *great songs*."

"No, of course not ..." his Dad ventured cautiously. "I was just mentioning. Totally unrelated."

"Oh, OK, cool." Arthur remembered to breathe. Usually Arthur cringed every time his dad mentioned *Lad Dadz*, but today he was actually interested.

His dad sat down next to Arthur and patted him on the shoulder. "Well, 'Fragile Dad Hearts' is one I wrote for a girl who broke my heart back in the nineties. Of course, back then it was just called 'Fragile Hearts' – you weren't even born! But these days we keep all our songs 'on brand', as you kids say." He winked. "Oh, and, 'Dads Heal In Time' – that was about a particularly nasty break-up . . ."

"What about Mum?" Arthur's eyes widened.

"Oh, well, when I met your mum suddenly love seemed easy. I haven't written an angsty song about her yet, after fifteen years of marriage. And I hope I never will!"

Hearing that made Arthur happy but, the thing was, he just found it so difficult to talk to girls – except Grace, because she was just a mate, but even that wasn't easy at the moment. Arthur wasn't like Kieran, who had girls falling at his feet left, right and centre. Arthur was worried.

"But what if it's never easy for me?" he asked.

But his dad just burst out laughing. "Oh, son. Don't worry. There's a lot for you to look forward to at the ripe old age of twelve."

Arthur tried to believe him. But even if he did manage to get through a sentence in front of a girl, how could he ever trust anyone again? He'd trusted Anna and she was probably the Summerby mole! He felt like such an idiot.

"Look," Arthur's dad carried on. "It will get better. Trust your old dad."

Arthur smiled and his dad got up. "Right, I'll leave you to your songs. I'll send you a link to 'Dads Heal In Time'." With a final pat on Arthur's shoulder, he left the room.

Arthur sat in silence. He glanced at the wig lying in the corner of his room. After seeing Anna's notes, he'd hardly listened to the rest of the FemSoc meeting. At one point he even realized that Esperanza had asked him a question and he hadn't noticed. Thankfully, everyone assumed his English wasn't good enough to understand and let him off the hook.

Afterwards he said as little as possible to Grace and Kieran, too. He'd just muttered that it was a FemSoc meeting, Diaz was no longer under suspicion and he hadn't found out anything. Thankfully, Grace was babbling excitedly once she'd realized Esperanza was the one in charge. Apparently, last year she'd got the local supermarkets to stop stocking animal-tested products. She was a shoo-in for Oxford University and she was, like, Grace's hero, or something. So in amongst listing all of Esperanza's achievements on the way home, no one noticed Arthur had barely said two words.

His phone buzzed. It was a message from Anna, suggesting that they help each other with their entries for the Park Protests competition. Pah! She didn't want to help him ... sabotage him, more like! Arthur sighed wistfully and deleted it.

There was another knock at the door. It was his older sister, Kirsty, this time. "Hey, lil bro," she said.

Arthur glanced around his room, at his dad's old heartbreak records strewn on the floor and the several empty tubs of ice cream. He must look really pitiable. She never called him "lil bro". "Some friends are here to see you ... Shall I tell them another time?"

Arthur cringed. He was still feeling too embarrassed to tell anyone about Anna, but he needed to come clean at some point, and they were here now. "Send them up," he said forlornly.

A few minutes later, Kieran's smiling face popped round the door.

"All right, mate!" He made his way across the room, stepping around all the heartbreak debris on the floor while kindly pretending not to see it. Grace followed him in.

"Are you OK, Arthur? We hadn't heard from you," Grace added.

Arthur took a deep breath, and ripped off the plaster. He told them all about what he'd seen in Anna's notebook.

To his surprise, Grace interrupted him and launched into a full-on rant. "Look, Arthur. I know I was the one who suspected Anna in the first place . . . but I've actually been thinking about everything long and hard. I think there might be more to the story, because . . ."

Arthur put his hands up. "Thanks for trying to spare my feelings, Grace, but it's not just the notebook."

Kieran and Grace looked at each other. "You found something else?" Kieran asked.

Arthur sighed, and braced himself to tell them what he'd discovered. His heart felt heavy. "When I got home, I searched through Anna's coverage online  looking for something that proved her innocence . . . but I ended up finding something that proved her guilt."

Kieran and Grace looked at each other and frowned. Instead of explaining, Arthur pulled out his laptop, opened up the *Anna's Amusings* website and found her coverage from the day of the Victory versus Summerby match four weeks ago. Then he opened a YouTube clip of the match that was filmed and uploaded by some eager parent.

"Look at this." He pressed play on both clips and synced them from the kick-off. Anna's bright, jokey voice filled the room. He cursed that the sound of it still made him want to skip and giggle and play with bunnies.

"*And after an unusual move, where Victory Road winger Grace Best cut inside and Lia Diakos ran around her, our Summerby defenders are straight in there tackling the ball away from Lia . . .*"

Arthur paused both videos. "Look," he instructed.

Grace and Kieran's eyes darted between the two screens. Arthur watched their mouths fall open as they saw what he was talking about. On the video the Summerby defenders had *only just* started to move. They hadn't tackled Lia yet and Anna was already commentating on it.

"She knew!" Kieran declared. "She'd been anticipating it!"

"Yup." Arthur sat back. His stomach felt like lead. Anna hadn't been reporting on what was happening; she'd been reporting on what she knew was *about* to happen … She knew how the Summerby team were planning to defend themselves from Victory Road's unusual tactics shift. She'd clearly spoken to the team about what Arthur had told her. His gut wrenched with guilt.

"OK, so, she knew what both teams were planning," Grace said. "That doesn't prove she's the one who *told* them what we were planning. You said you didn't tell her anything, right? Even if she was taking notes about you … what would she have found out?"

Arthur's heart started pounding. His shoulders tensed. This was it – the moment he lost his best mates, on top of the girl he liked. But he deserved it. He'd let his heart overrule his head in this investigation. He'd been a fool. Now he understood what the saying "love is blind" meant. (He'd heard that from Grace's dad, who was always coming out with wise, cryptic titbits)

"I lied," he said under his breath. His mouth was

so dry. "I let slip what we were planning. I guess I wanted to impress her. There's nothing I can say to make this better, but please believe me when I say I really didn't think this would happen."

Grace looked shocked. Kieran looked unbearably disappointed. But no more disappointed than Arthur was in himself.

There was a moment of silence. "Do you hate me?" Arthur asked.

Now Grace and Kieran looked less shocked and disappointed . . . and more confused.

"Hate you?" Kieran repeated. "Why would we *hate* you?"

"Because I let you down. I let the school down." Arthur couldn't stand how choked up he sounded.

Kieran and Grace looked at each other and back at Arthur, and shook their heads. "No, mate, I'm just sad you lied. You could've told us. But none of this is your fault."

"Yeah, Arthur," Grace added. "Everyone makes mistakes."

Arthur looked up at his two best mates, his heart filling with relief and joy. They didn't hate him. He still had friends.

"I still think there's more to this story," Grace went on. "OK, so, you told Anna about *one* match. But how did—"

"Grace, it's nice of you," Arthur interrupted. "But the answer's plain as day. It's Anna. I'm sorry, but I don't feel like continuing this investigation. I can't do it. You two go on, though. Smash it with a huge scoop, yeah? I'll cheer you on from the sidelines."

Grace and Kieran looked at each other again. Arthur seemed more dispirited than they'd ever seen him.

"All right, mate," Kieran leaned in for a hug. "Talk soon, yeah?"

Arthur nodded, and Grace and Kieran left.

It seemed wise not to press him today, but how on earth were they supposed to carry on without Arthur?

CHAPTER ELEVEN

> KIERAN (coughing over the last few words of the jingle) ... er hi yeah ... You're listening to *Radio Royalty*, but it's just me ... yeah ... once again, I'll, er ... be flying solo today ...

Grace switched off the radio in the girls' locker rooms. She couldn't bear to listen to Kieran present another show without Arthur. Kieran was a great presenter in his own right, but the two of them just had something together that was hard for Kieran to recreate as a one-man band.

"It's not as funny without Arthur, is it?" Grace heard one girl say, as she shoved her football gear back into a bag.

"No. I've been listening to *Best of the Best* all week instead. I'm not liking *Radio Royalty's* chances of winning the Park Protests competition ..."

Grace cringed. A few months ago, before she became friends with Arthur and Kieran, she would have relished their diminished chances of winning the competition. Now, not only would beating them feel like a hollow victory, but she actually felt sad for them.

Grace had been feeling down all week. The only times she managed to distract herself was in training, like today, or by preparing her Park Protests competition entry. On paper, she should be feeling pleased. She'd suspected Anna all along and now here was evidence pointing to her as the Summerby mole. But she'd had a chance to think everything over, and nothing was adding up. Even if Arthur *had* told Anna about that one match, what about all the other suspicious circumstances – including all the Victory Road losses *before* Arthur and Anna had even met? Anna didn't have any other known links to Victory Road apart from Arthur. Not that Grace was aware of, anyway.

And Grace had to force herself to question why she'd been so determined to believe the worst in Anna from the start. Why was she so willing to point the finger at her when she had no solid reason to be suspicious in the first place?

Grace swallowed down a nauseous feeling. It might be time to confront the truth. It might be that . . . oh, she couldn't even bring herself to *think* it, it was too weird . . . Could it be possible that *she* fancied Arthur?!

Her rising sense of being sick in her own mouth, a bit like that time she ate some bad jolly rice, made it quickly very obvious that the answer was *no*. Not in a million years. He's just a mate. And also totally gross. And annoying. And she'd rather lick her brothers' nasty socks that had been left on the bathroom floor than entertain the idea of fancying him.

So that was definitely a no, then.

But she couldn't deny how determined she'd been that Anna was guilty – even without any evidence, which was so unlike her practical, logical self. There *must* be some reason for it.

Lia patted her on the shoulder. "Are you all right, Grace? You look a bit … green about the gills."

"Oh, I'm … fine," Grace lied.

Lia raised an eyebrow. She wasn't buying it for a second and neither were the rest of the team, who had overheard Lia's question and were looking at Grace with concerned eyes.

"Are you thinking about the Park Protests contest?" she asked. "When's the deadline? In a few days, right?"

Grace nodded. She'd nearly finished her entry, which consisted of two radio clips as well as an article, just to show she was versatile. She was nervous, particularly thinking about what Michael and Anna might have prepared. Anna was so funny, and Michael was more experienced in print than she was. As if the stress of all that wasn't enough. She wished the competition was the *only* thing on her mind!

"If you don't want to talk about it then that's totally fine," Lia said. "But you know you can trust us, right?"

Grace looked around the group of girls, who had all stopped what they were doing and crowded around her, and felt a rush of warmth. Joining the girls' football team had been one of the best decisions she'd ever made. The team weren't just there for her on the pitch, but off it as well. It was different from her friendship with Arthur and Kieran. Growing up with two brothers, Grace was still getting used to having female friends. And though she knew she could talk to Arthur and Kieran about anything, there was just something so uplifting about a large group of girls fiercely having your back.

"I ... I'm trying to work out ..." Grace gulped. Could she share this? Would they laugh at her? Would they tell everyone? *What if Arthur found out?* She thought about making up some tale about forgetting her homework, or having got a bad mark. But looking into Lia's eyes made her feel secure. Cautiously, she told the truth. "Whether I like one of my friends ... as more than a friend," she finished.

Lia didn't even blink. "OK, this friend. Do you get butterflies around them?"

Grace looked blank.

"Like . . . fluttering in your tummy?"

"Urgh, no!" Grace shook her head.

"Do you get nervous around them?"

"*No.*" The corner of her lip curled humorously at the thought of being *nervous* around Arthur. She was usually bossing him around.

"Do you dream about them?"

Grace thought for a second. "Hmm, I once had a dream I beat them in the World Olympics. And another dream I beat them at horseriding, oh, and bowling—"

"If they were to walk into the room right now and you were eating something hot," Lia interrupted, "would you be distracted and forget to blow, then burn your mouth?"

"Errr . . . no I manage to eat around them just fine . . ."

Lia held a hand up to stop Grace talking. She looked at the other girls, who all appeared

baffled. "What *is* it that makes you think you
might like this person, Grace?"

"They, er, well, they made this other
friend, and I . . ." Grace felt heat rising in her
cheeks. It was *so* embarrassing to admit. ". . . I
got jealous."

Lia grinned. "Oh my God, Grace, that's *so*
normal. It doesn't mean you like-like them."

"It doesn't?" Grace asked, feeling her whole
body relax.

"No!" Lia looked at the other girls, who were smiling and nodding their heads. Grace felt her anxiety melting away. It seemed like everyone knew exactly what she meant.

"When my friend changed schools, I got so jealous of the pictures of her and her new friends, I had to stop looking at them," said one girl.

"Yeah, me and my best mate used to watch anime together, and then she made this other mate who loved anime. I got so worried that she knew more about anime than me and that they'd watch it without me," said another girl.

Everyone was nodding. Suddenly, something clicked in Grace's brain. Not only had Arthur made a new friend, he'd made a new friend with a *kick-ass radio show*. She didn't like-like Arthur ... She liked *competing* with Arthur! The radio, and trying to beat each other in the ratings, was *their* thing. Somewhere in Grace's mind it must have felt like Anna was taking that away from her.

Grace breathed a huge sigh of relief. This made *so* much more sense than fancying him! He slouched and had messy hair and *holes in his socks*. A great pal, but . . . *ewww*.

"You're so right!" Grace giggled at how ridiculous it was that she'd even thought it. "Thank you so much. I don't know what I was thinking!"

Lia shrugged. "Sometimes it's hard to work out how you're feeling without talking to someone."

Lia was totally right. Since hanging out with the girls on the team *and* since working alongside Arthur and Kieran, Grace had experienced how nice it felt to share a problem now and again. She was so used to having all the answers that she still expected to work everything out for herself. But it seemed like working out your own emotions could be even more difficult than a tricky investigation!

Lia took her hand and gave it a little squeeze as all the girls carried on getting changed and putting their kits away. Grace felt like a huge weight had been lifted off her shoulders.

She picked up her phone to tell her parents she was en route home, when she saw something. She'd been looking at the *Anna's Amusings* website earlier, and the tab was still open. Anna had uploaded a picture of herself by the pond in Greenfair Park, with the caption "doing some research for Friday's *Wildlife Weekly* segment!" It was posted ten minutes ago.

Grace knew what she had to do. There was still something more to this story and she was determined to find out what. And this time she wasn't going to let her emotions get in the way.

CHAPTER TWELVE

[Intro: Jungle noises, cue "The Lion Sleeps Tonight".]

ANNA: And welcome to *Anna's Amusings'* Wildlife Weekly! As requested, listeners have kindly sent me their animal impressions, which I'll be playing throughout the show. Correct guesses go into my Friday prize draw! OK, let's start with one of my faves — this is Jimmy Thompson from Year 4:

JIMMY: Wraaarrghhhhhwrrrrrhhhhh

ANNA: One more time ...

JIMMY: Wraaarrghhhhhwrrrrrhhhhh

ANNA: There you go! Let me know what you think it is ... Get in touch by text/email/

Twitter, you know the drill, and you could
be our winner! And while you do that I'll be
in Greenfair Park, looking at all the local
animals that could sadly lose their homes if
the development of luxury flats goes ahead . . .

Grace watched Anna from the edge of the
park. Anna was holding a newt, which Grace
assumed would be animal number one. This
was such a smart idea! Grace inwardly cursed,
wishing she'd thought of this for *her* Park Protest
entry. The deadline was looming, and Anna's
entry was clearly going to give her a run for her
money! Were the shows Grace had recorded
good enough? Should she rerecord her sports
coverage? But then, she wanted to use one of the
matches that had been played in Greenfair Park,
to keep it themed . . . Ugh, now wasn't the time
to focus on this! Grace had a job to do.

On the way over she'd been frantically

plotting how to get the truth out of Anna ...
and after thinking through multiple wacky
scenarios, including bribery with a lifetime
supply of Snickers (Arthur had once said it was
her favourite chocolate bar), Grace knew that,
really, the bottom line was that she *needed* to get
a proper look in that notebook.

Grace took a deep breath and headed
towards Anna.

"Hi, Anna," she called, giving her an
awkward wave.

Anna stopped recording and turned off her
microphone. "Hi, Grace," she replied. Grace
noticed instantly that she didn't have the same
boldness or banter that she usually did. Grace
had heard that while listening to Anna's recent
shows, too. Maybe she was gutted that Arthur
wasn't talking to her any more? Even if she *had*
used him for information, it seemed like she
missed hanging out with him too.

"I've just come to ask you a few questions, if that's OK?" Grace began. "I'm doing a segment on female comedians." She glanced down at Anna's bag and saw the top of the red notebook peeking out. *Bingo.*

Anna smiled. "Well, thanks for including me."

"You're first on my list." Grace beamed. She did actually want to do a segment on this. Esperanza and FemSoc had inspired her to promote more talented girls on her show.

"So, will you be doing your classic comedy style for your Park Protests entry, or will you be going for a more serious vibe?" Grace's stomach lurched thinking about the competition.

"Wouldn't you like to know." Anna tapped her nose.

Grace smirked. Of course she wasn't going to give anything away. "I'm sure listeners would love to know how you come up with your jokes," Grace went on. "Do you prepare them beforehand or do they just hit you?"

"You mean, like, in the face?" Anna joked.

Grace could see why Arthur and Anna got on so well. He never took questions seriously, either.

Just then, the newt in Anna's hand started to wriggle. "Hang on, let me just put this little guy down for a moment," she said.

"What is he?" Grace asked. Her wildlife knowledge was woefully lacking.

"He's a smooth newt. Given that it's springtime i.e. newt breeding season, he's feeling *especially* 'smooth' today. Classic grey-brown, with an orange belly and black spots all over. He's a big one, though! About fifteen centimetres. They're usually only ten."

"Oh, wow, so he's a super-smooth newt," Grace commented.

Anna laughed. "Yes, that's good. Mind if I use that?"

"Sure." Grace was secretly pleased. "So anyway, back to you. What got you into comedy?"

"My mum's a stand up," Anna answered. "She goes to Edinburgh Fringe every year."

"Really?" *That's so cool,* thought Grace. She reminded herself not to get sidetracked. She was here to get a look in that notebook, somehow!

"So do you take notes?" Grace asked, glancing at the notebook. "About things that make you laugh during the week? Or little jokes that you come up with?"

"Erm, yes." Anna followed Grace's gaze. "Yes, I do . . ." Her voice wavered. She suddenly sounded more guarded. *There are definitely secrets hidden in that book,* thought Grace.

Sensing her protectiveness over the book, Grace's plan A of asking Anna to show her some jokes, taking the book out of her hands then "accidentally" flipping the pages, was out of the window. She'd have to move to plan B: waiting until Anna was distracted and sneaking a peek. Her heart thudded. This was *much* more risky. It was usually Arthur who got sent in to do things like that. This was *way* out of her comfort zone.

She continued interviewing Anna for ten minutes or so, then brought it to a close.

"Thanks so much for chatting with us, Anna. *Best of the Best* listeners will be super interested to hear your advice on comedy."

"Well . . . if '*be as silly as possible at all times*' counts as advice then I'm happy to help." Anna grinned.

Grace laughed. "OK, see you, Anna."

"Bye, Grace." There was something unspoken in Anna's eyes. Grace guessed Anna might be stopping herself from asking after Arthur. But she couldn't let herself get distracted.

Grace said goodbye and made to exit the park. As she was walking through Greenfair, a ball rolled towards her and she kicked it lazily back to a group of children playing. The sun was shining and Grace felt a confusing mix of emotions: joy at how beautiful the park was and anger about what they were planning to do to it. Where were all the kids supposed to go and play? What about the wildlife? The park was such an important part of the community, she couldn't bear the thought of losing it. Grace felt a surge of excitement about putting the finishing touches to her competition entry pieces this evening. She wanted so badly to be the one who helped raise awareness of the protests.

Grace left through the gates and then, when Anna had turned back to the pond and started recording her wildlife segment again, she dashed back in. Hiding behind various bushes and groups of kids, she made her way back along the grass until she got to a good vantage point.

Grace waited, and watched. From a distance Anna looked a bit bonkers, standing on her own doing animal impressions. It appeared she liked to act them out even though her listeners couldn't see her. She didn't seem to care about all the odd looks she was attracting, and it crossed Grace's mind again how similar Anna was to Arthur. She realized that, for his sake, she sort of hoped Anna was innocent.

After crouching behind some shrubs for what felt like the longest time, Grace finally spotted her moment as Anna began heading for the toilet. She took her purse, microphone and equipment, presumably to keep them safe, but left her bag by the side of the pond.

Grace felt like she might faint, she was so nervous. What if someone saw her and accused her of being a thief? What if she tripped over when she was running away? There were a million things that could go wrong! But Grace only had two minutes or so before Anna would be back from the loo. There was no time to dither.

She made a break for it.

Reaching Anna's bag, Grace's hands were trembling so much she thought she might actually drop the notebook in the pond. She took a deep breath and got ready to flick through the pages.

But suddenly . . . it all felt so wrong. As Grace held Anna's private notebook in her hands, she realized she couldn't open it. It was one thing sneaking into Alan the caretaker's hut, or dressing up as a French exchange student, but invading someone's privacy? What if Anna had written really personal things in here? Grace shuddered to think what someone might find if they opened *her* old diaries. She thought of her football team. If they could see her now, they'd all be shaking their heads and telling her in no uncertain terms to put the book back.

Grace had been here before. Being a journalist, sometimes it was hard to work out the line between right and wrong. But even though she was seeking the truth, it wasn't OK to hack Anna's private information. She exhaled and shakily replaced the notebook. She'd have to find some other way to investigate.

But at that very moment a shadow fell over her. Grace's blood went cold. *Please . . . please don't let that be . . .*

Anna's voice sounded from behind her. "Grace? What are you doing?"

Grace gulped.

CHAPTER THIRTEEN

> **GRACE:** Aaaand in today's episode of *You Got Punked*, I attempt to put a fake dead mouse in an unsuspecting Anna Fong's bag . . .

But Anna wasn't buying it for a second. She stood, staring aghast at Grace. "Pffft." She snorted. "Nice try. You don't have a prank segment on *Best of the Best*, Grace. Playful isn't exactly your style. Why were you *really* looking in my bag?"

Grace began sweating. She took a deep breath.

"It's not what it looks like," she garbled.

"So, you weren't reading my private notebook?" Anna asked.

"OK, so, it is a *bit* what it looks like," Grace admitted. "I was *going* to. But then I didn't. I promise!"

Anna nodded. It seemed like she tentatively believed her. "What were you trying to find?" she asked.

Here was the moment. The moment to make something else up. Some excuse … But everything she'd learned from her team made her wonder if there was another way to go about this. So Grace tried talking to Anna like Lia talked to her the other day.

"Arthur's upset because it looks like you've been using things he tells you to help Summerby win everything. I just wanted to find out, for Arthur's sake, if it was true. But I know now that looking in your private stuff isn't the way to do that." Grace talked quickly.

"Is *that* why Arthur's stopped replying to me?"

Anna seemed genuinely surprised. It looked as if she didn't have a clue about the plot against Victory Road. She was either innocent or a *very* good liar. But then, how *did* she know what Summerby were going to do at that match, if she hadn't been conspiring with them about Victory Road's secret plan?

"When we listened back over some of your old coverage, it seemed like you knew how Summerby were going to defend against Victory Road, before they actually did it," Grace explained. "We assumed you must have told the Summerby team about our top secret change of tactics ... the change of tactics that, um, Arthur told you in confidence."

Anna's lip quivered and her eyes started watering. *Oh no*, Grace thought. Why was she crying? Was it because she was being falsely accused, or because she had something terrible to hide? Grace prayed it was the former.

To Grace's surprise, Anna reached down and pulled out her notebook. She flipped to the page with *Arthur* written at the top and shoved it towards Grace.

"Are you sure?" Grace asked.

Anna nodded.

Grace began reading. "Oh . . ." she said, as she took in the words.

All that was written there were snippets and advice about radio. From silly things to help with nerves like "pretend everyone in the audience is wearing socks as mittens", that Anna had clearly found funny, to more serious tips about how Arthur interviewed people and how to get the best out of them. Grace recognized a few herself, that she'd also learned from Arthur months ago.

"I wasn't writing down *insider information*

for Summerby," Anna sniffed. "I would never betray Arthur like that. I was just writing down tips. I was so excited to meet another radio presenter. There aren't very many at Summerby. Michael is a brilliant journalist but, well, he doesn't exactly share. Look . . . I have a Grace page as well."

Anna flipped a few pages forward and showed her the "Grace page", with a few things written down from their brief conversations. There were notes like "intellect", "meticulous research" (meticulous was even underlined) and "warmth". Grace felt herself flush.

"I just want to be the best radio journalist I can be," Anna went on. "Sometimes . . . well, sometimes I get worried *funny* is the only style I can do. You and Arthur, and Kieran, are all so versatile. I just wanted to learn everything I could."

Grace shone with pride. That was such

a compliment, coming from someone as talented as Anna.

"This is really lovely," she said tentatively. "But how did you get Summerby's strategy so bang on if you never even talked to them about what Victory Road were planning?"

Anna cast her eyes downward. "This is *really* embarrassing," she confessed. "... I looked at Michael's notes. Sports journalism is my weakest area, and I thought Michael might have some extra research to help me prepare. Then I saw that he had lots of gameplay written down. Somehow he knew Victory's secret plan, *and* Summerby's secret counter plan."

Grace's eyes darted from side to side, processing this new information. *Michael knew everything.* But how? They'd basically written him off because Michael's only known link to Victory Road was Diaz. And Michael seemed like a typical loner at Summerby. So where would he get his tip-offs?

"I swear I didn't tell either team anything!" Anna continued, blushing.

"Why didn't you say anything afterwards?" Grace asked.

Anna looked really upset. "Because then everyone would know what I'd done. I knew it was cheating, but . . . oh, I really want to win this Park Protests competition, Grace. I mean, *local radio.*" Her eyes glimmered with ambition. Grace knew the feeling. "I would never betray a friend, I mean, an Arthur, I mean . . . you know what I mean," Anna fumbled.

And Grace did. She understood what it was like to want something so much that you'd do anything – maybe even cheat a bit – to get it. "I understand," Grace reassured her. "We all make mistakes we're not proud of. I almost looked in your private diary!"

Anna smiled. "But you didn't."

Grace smiled back.

As she left Anna to finish her wildlife segment, for real this time, Grace messaged Kieran and asked him to come over to her house. They had a brand new prime suspect to investigate. Serious Michael Bernard of *Summerby Stories* . . . but just *where* was he getting his information?

***

Grace threw Michael's article on the *Greenfair's Got Talent* acts down on the table, her spirits soaring in the way they only did when she'd hit on some true journalistic gold. After hours of sitting and rereading every last piece of Michael's coverage for the past few months, they'd finally, *finally* got something. She pointed at the evidence in question and put her right hand on Kieran's shoulder. He put his left hand on hers.

*Strictly Summerby, choreographed by
Danza Studios, is set to make a splash with a
unique blend of jazz, tap and modern . . .*

It was an early profile on all the entries
submitting for the show. There were over a
hundred performers, before they got narrowed
down. This piece was published months before
Greenfair's Got Talent.

*Victory Road's dance troupe, spearheaded
by Lia Diakos, will be sporting matching
black V-necks and top hats for their number.
Choreographed by Danza Studios . . .*

"Choreographed by Danza Studios!
Choreographed by Danza Studios!" Grace
yelled, stabbing her finger at both profiles.
They'd done it! They'd found a lead! Obviously,
Anna's admission about seeing Michael's notes

was solid evidence, but she had begged Grace not to share that fact with anyone. Plus, even though they now trusted Anna, they only really had her word for it. It wouldn't be enough to prove anything ... but this would.

"How did he know?" Kieran shouted. "How did he know what choreographer the teams were using? This piece was printed *way* before any of that was revealed."

Grace shook her head in disbelief that she hadn't noticed this before. She'd read all of Michael's articles on *Greenfair's Got Talent* – in fact, she'd read all of Michael's articles, full stop! – but it was incredible how much you could miss if you didn't know what you were looking for. But there was no way Michael could explain this away. This piece was printed prior to the show. And no one else had worked it out until Anna broke the news on *Anna's Amusings*. So how on earth did Michael know about it?

"He *knew*," Grace asserted. "And he kept it a secret!"

"I suppose it's possible he didn't think it was a big deal that both teams were using the same choreographer?" Kieran suggested.

But Grace shook her head. "With his eye for detail, I don't think so. Plus, when the Double Dance Disaster happened, why was *Anna* the one to break the news? Michael had it sitting there in his archives all along! He knew ... and he didn't want anyone to know that he knew!"

Kieran's eyes were darting from side to side. It was all a bit confusing. "Mind. Blown," he said, touching his hands to his heads and then throwing them up. "So he knew about Victory Road's tactic change *and* Summerby's line of defence at the football match. And he knew what choreographer the teams were using at GGT." Kieran listed off the facts on his fingers.

"He has information from both sides. But where's he getting it?"

Grace shrugged, exasperated. "I don't know."

There was a soft knocking at the door. Arthur had arrived. Grace and Kieran were bursting to tell him everything they'd discovered. With Arthur having insisted he was out of the investigation, they'd had to lure him over with the promise of Grace's mum's delicious home cooking and a game of Monopoly. But they were *sure* he'd be back in after they told him what they'd discovered.

They filled him in on everything, including Grace and Anna's conversation at the park. After they'd finished, Arthur sat back in awe.

"So . . . Anna didn't tell the Summerby team what I told her?"

Grace shook her head. "Nope."

Kieran and Grace looked at each other. They'd expected Arthur to be happy to learn that Anna was innocent, but he looked stricken.

"Yup." Grace nodded, responding to the guilt that she felt sure Arthur was feeling for not only thinking the worst of Anna but also ignoring her.

Suddenly, there was a pounding on the door. Grace's brothers, Lucas and Nathan, came tumbling in. "Mum says the Suya is ready if you all want some."

Kieran's eyes lit up. Grace smiled. It was funny to think that a few months ago she would have cringed at her mum offering Arthur and Kieran Nigerian food.

"Great, thanks," Grace said.

Grace noted with satisfaction that her brothers were clearly trying to peer at her computer. They used to make fun of her investigations, but ever since she, Arthur and Kieran landed the biggest scoop in Victory Road High's history –

the stolen trophy's return – they'd shown her a lot more respect. And this investigation could lead to an *even bigger* scoop. Someone potentially using classified information to fix multiple inter-school competitions ... Grace could only *imagine* the ratings that would come once they exposed the culprit. They'd have two different schools tuning in!

"How's your entry for the Park Protests Contest going?" Lucas asked, still nosying at her screen.

"None of your beeswax," Grace answered. She rubbed her hands together with glee at the thought of winning. Her brothers would *never* be able to make fun of her show ever again once she had been on the actual radio. Although, if she was really honest with herself, she wasn't *totally* confident about her entry. She understood why they were only allowed to submit material from the last two months, so as not to favour kids who already had up-and-running papers and radio shows. But that had made it particularly challenging. Over the years, she had stored up plenty of amazing material, but over the past few months – with all the losses and negative energy at Victory Road – she hadn't created as much to be proud of.

"All right, all right, chill your beans," said Nathan, turning to leave the room. "We're just being *supportive brothers.*"

"How *is* everyone feeling about the deadline?" Kieran asked once they'd gone.

Arthur wavered his hand back and forth to indicate "so-so". They had the exact same concern that Grace did. "I can't believe it came around so fast. It's like, yesterday it was *two months ago,* and now it's here."

Suddenly, Arthur stood up and grabbed the competition flyer from Grace's desk. "Argh!" he shouted. "We missed it. *We missed it.*"

"No we didn't, it's tomorrow," said Kieran.

"No, we missed *the motive*." Arthur pointed to the flyer. "When did Victory Road start mysteriously losing to Summerby, Grace?"

"About two months ago," Grace answered.

"And when was this competition announced?"

"About two ..." Grace caught Arthur's meaning and stopped mid-sentence.

Kieran took the flyer out of Arthur's hands, shaking his head. "We've been colossal doughnuts," he said.

"Michael doesn't just want Summerby to beat Victory Road at everything; this is about *him* and his coverage. He wants to win the Park Protests Competition," Grace whispered.

CHAPTER FOURTEEN

[Intro: Tension music (3 secs).]

KIERAN: Hi, everyone. After months of waiting and tense anticipation, it all comes down to this. There are less than ten minutes to go for budding young journalists of Greenfair to get their entries in, to be in with a chance of covering the Park Protests this weekend for Greenfair FM ... And now, Arthur McLean steps up to the laptop ... He wipes a bead of sweat from his furrowed brow ... aaand presses the upload button ... There's no going back now, Radio Royalty's entry is away! With only

eight minutes to go, next to submit is the
fearless Grace Best, presenter of Listen Up's
other show, Best Of The Best. Seven minutes
and counting . . .

Kieran wasn't just saying it for dramatic effect,
Arthur actually *was* sweating. It was deadline
day and the entries had to be in by twelve
p.m. Somehow, with everything that had been
going on, Arthur had managed to push this
out of his mind. It seemed more important to
try and catch whoever had been rigging every
competition between Summerby and Victory
Road. But he still badly wanted to win, and he
couldn't ignore the nagging feeling that they'd
played perfectly into Michael's hands.

Arthur and Kieran had listened back to
their entries earlier. There was no denying it,
with everything that had been going on, it
wasn't their best. Still, they'd all managed to

cobble together something decent, and Arthur prayed that it would be enough. Maybe their natural talents could still shine through and win the day.

Arthur's mind wandered to Anna. He hoped she felt more confident about her entry than they did. She was so talented, and was surely in with a good chance of winning. Especially given what Grace had said about her clever *Wildlife Weekly* segment in Greenfair Park.

"How are we going to wait until *next week* to find out who wins?" Kieran wailed.

"My dad says patience is a virtue," Grace answered, chewing a piece of her hair. Arthur smirked. He wasn't sure that particular saying had rubbed off on Grace.

Arthur clapped his hands together. "Look, there's nothing we can do about our entries now, but I've been thinking. We *can* do something about Michael's."

"What do you mean?" Grace stopped chewing.

"At the moment, we only have proof he *knows* things. We need proof that he's actually *involved* in playing the schools against each other. If we can prove Michael's behind all the recent losses and that he was cheating, then *surely* they'd have to disqualify his entry?"

At that, Grace's eyes lit up. "Oh my goodness, Arthur, you're right!"

"Does this mean ...?" Kieran asked tentatively.

Arthur nodded. "I'm back in the investigation."

Grace and Kieran breathed a sigh of relief. Kieran put his hands together like he was thanking a higher being. They'd made mistakes, and they'd missed what now seemed like a very *obvious* motive, but Arthur was back in, and they were going to solve this together.

Arthur pulled a piece of paper out of his

pocket. "And I know just where to start: Danza Studios . . ."

***

Thankfully, the studio wasn't too far from Grace's house.

"Last night," Arthur explained as they walked, "I spoke to Tilly-Mae and Lia about both the Summerby *and* Victory Road dance teams. So, Victory Road *booked* the choreographer, but Summerby were contacted by Danza Studios *directly*. The studio *called them* to say they were returning an initial enquiry, but they never actually made one."

"That's strange . . ." Grace said as she walked briskly. "So Strictly Summerby didn't book the choreographer themselves . . ."

"Well, they did. But only after Danza Studios got in touch. Tilly-Mae said it was super weird that a brilliant, affordable dance studio with a great reputation had rung them at exactly the time they were looking for a choreographer. They thought it was fate."

"Someone *wanted* both teams to go there," Grace concluded.

"Exactly." Arthur nodded. "All we need is proof that Michael made that initial enquiry," he went on. "It wasn't a coincidence, I'm sure of it. I have a hunch that Michael planned it. The question is: how?"

"But how do we find that out?" Grace asked. "We can't exactly just walk in and say, excuse me, who made this random booking months ago?"

Arthur shrugged. "I think we have to. It's the only lead we've got."

When they arrived, they had to wait for half an hour for the teacher to finish a salsa class. She was a petite, Argentine woman with long, flowing hair that twirled as she moved. As Arthur, Grace and Kieran watched her through the window, they could see how both teams would have thought it was their lucky day when she phoned them. Her routines were *amazing*. Arthur started trying to join in, but once he'd tripped over Grace's foot and taken them both down in a heap, they begged him to stop.

When the class ended, they approached the teacher while she was stretching and drinking water in preparation for her next session.

"Hi," Grace ventured, reaching her hand out. "I'm Grace Best."

"Hello, dear, I'm Sofia." Sofia took Grace's hand. Her eyes twinkled with humour at the formal introduction.

"We were wondering if we could ..."

"My dear, your posture," interrupted Sofia. "We'll have to work on that. But I can already tell you'd have excellent footwork."

"Oh, no," Grace giggled. "I'm not a *dancer*, I . . ."

"Not yet, anyway," Sofia winked. "I know potential when I see it."

Grace briefly imagined herself moving elegantly across a stage in front of hundreds of people . . . maybe a challenge for *after* she conquered the radio world.

"Anyway," Arthur coughed. "Amazing dancing, Sofia." Sofia shot him a dazzling smile.

"We're doing a piece on dancing in schools, and we wondered if you remember two groups from Summerby Secondary and Victory Road High, a few weeks ago?"

Suddenly, Sofia's face dropped. "Ah, the Double Dance Disaster," she muttered. "Most unfortunate. My daughter goes to Summerby. A terrible tragedy."

"We were wondering if you could tell us who made the initial . . ." Arthur started.

But Sofia's mood had instantly shifted. "I'm afraid my daughter handles all the bookings and anyway, I couldn't tell you anything," she answered shortly. "Data protection. Ah, my next group is starting to arrive. If you'd like to sign up then do contact us through our website." With that, she'd tapped off into the studio, and that was the end of the conversation.

Kieran, Arthur and Grace replayed it over and over, but they couldn't find any clues. Sofia was clearly upset by the Double Dance Disaster. As soon as that had come up, it was as if the shutters slammed down.

"If only we could have asked who her daughter was." Kieran sighed. "Then we might have a clue."

Suddenly, Arthur's eyes widened. "Daughter," he repeated slowly.

Grace and Kieran both stared at him as Arthur rushed to his laptop and opened up the recording of when he went undercover at FemSoc. He pressed play about halfway in.

"My mother's a dance teacher . . ."

"The girl who led FemSoc at Summerby!" Arthur cried. "I knew it!"

Kieran pointed at Arthur. "YES! ARTHUR!" he shouted.

"Esperanza?" Grace was getting excited.

"Grace, what's Esperanza's last name?" Arthur asked.

"Morales!" Grace was bursting with excitement. She was already on her phone, looking at social media. Her eyes lit up. She turned her phone round and Arthur and Kieran both stared at it. She had googled "Sofia Morales, dance teacher" and there was a picture of Sofia, standing beneath the "Danza Studios" sign.

"She's definitely Esperanza's mum!" Grace cried.

Kieran started jumping around, then kissed his hands and raised them in the air. Arthur smiled, pleased that Grace's idolization of Esperanza had paid off. Sofia obviously wasn't going to help them, but her daughter might.

CHAPTER FIFTEEN

[Intro: *Best of the Best* jingle (7 secs).]

GRACE: Good morning Victory Road, it's Grace Best with you on Listen Up! Now, we know exam term is looming for many of you, so please welcome a very special guest to today's edition of *Best of the Best*: 'Your Future Career.' Joining me is Summerby FemSoc president and animal rights activist Esperanza Morales. Earlier this week I asked for your questions, and I'm really excited to hear Esperanza's answers! Let's get the ball rolling with this question from Miko in Year 5. Esperanza, what's the best *and* worst thing about setting up a campaign . . .?

Grace's voice was wobbling. She couldn't believe she was interviewing Esperanza. This girl had *single-handedly* had all animal-tested products banned from their local supermarket. She'd started so many societies at Summerby, Grace was surprised she didn't have five arms to juggle everything with. She had an offer from Oxford University and was on a fast track to a career in politics.

Esperanza had agreed over email to meet with them and they'd had to rush over to Summerby after the school day ended. They only had *ten minutes* before Esperanza had FemSoc, so it was going to be tight.

"So, Esperanza, when the local supermarket agreed to stop stocking animal-tested products as a direct result of your campaign, what did that *feel* like?" Grace asked.

"Amazing," Esperanza answered. "Some might say it's just a small victory, but I don't like to think of it that way. Bigger victories are built on lots of smaller ones. If everyone fought for more small victories, then combined they can lead to huge change."

Grace grinned. One minute into talking with Esperanza and she was already feeling like the power of her voice was limitless.

"That's such a good way to look at it," Grace said. "If everyone thought that their own victories were *only small*, so stopped trying, we'd never change anything."

Esperanza laughed. "Well, exactly. The only thing that's pointless is people believing their actions are pointless."

Grace beamed. Kieran and Arthur were sitting beside her, completely caught up in their conversation. It was hard not to be absorbed by Esperanza's inspirational words.

"So how are you feeling about next week's protests at Greenfair Park?" Grace asked. "Need I ask what side you're on?"

"As you might have guessed, I'm against the luxury flat development," Esperanza said. "For all the usual reasons: the impact on the environment and the effect on the local community. This is especially personal for me, as not only did I play in that park as a child – like everyone around here – but my mother's business also depends heavily on that park. She owns a dance studio nearby. As soon as you lose the park, you lose business."

Grace pulled a face. "I hadn't thought of that."

"The developer's argument is that more people living in the area means more custom. But if you look at the amount of people who travel to, and use, the park, versus the amount of people you can fit in a building of large, luxury apartments, that argument doesn't make any sense." Esperanza inhaled to soothe herself. This was obviously an emotional topic for her, as it was for everyone in the area.

"I'm so proud of my mum ..." Esperanza sniffed. "Starting your own business is hard. Not to mention in something like dance. It's her passion, but it isn't exactly dependable. I dread to think what will happen if the park is demolished, I really do. And it's not just my mum's business. Many businesses will suffer."

Esperanza got out a list of people whose businesses and jobs would be impacted. From the obvious places like the cafes and shops on the edge of the park, to all the places like Esperanza's mother's business that relied on the footfall the park attracted.

Grace was speechless. If she was honest, beyond no longer having a place for herself and her friends to play in the sunshine, she hadn't *really* thought about the impact of the park being gone. But over the past few weeks, it turned out there was so much more to it. Anna had made her think about the impact on the environment, and now this … It could really threaten people's livelihoods. Grace had cared about the park protests before, but now she felt even more passionately about being the one to help spread their message.

"So, speaking of your mum's business, is that something you're involved in at all?" Grace adopted an innocent expression.

"I do some of the back office stuff, the boring admin," Esperanza answered.

"So what does that involve? Like … bookings and stuff?"

Arthur winked at her from behind Esperanza. Grace couldn't help but feel pleased with herself. Chatting to interviewees and drawing them out was more Arthur and Kieran's thing, but since they'd become friends she'd learned a thing or two from them.

"Yes, I do the bookings," said Esperanza. "But I think you already knew that, didn't you?" She cocked her head to one side and raised an eyebrow.

. . .Or not.

Grace's chest felt tight. "Er, I . . ."

"It's nice to see you again, by the way . . . *Pierre McFrance*." Esperanza turned around to Arthur and winked.

Arthur nearly fell off of his chair. He swallowed some water the wrong way and started coughing. Kieran thumped him on the back and laughed uproariously.

"Oh, this isn't Pierre . . . This is, um, Pierre's English cousin . . . Your aunt's French, isn't she, Arthur?"

"Quick thinking," said Esperanza. "But you

don't fool me. I saw you two walking away from school with Pierre, and the ginger wig was missing right before the Year 7 production of *Harry Potter*. Ron Weasley had to be blonde! Then my mum told me about three radio kids from Victory Road who just happened to want to start dance lessons yesterday."

Kieran paled, and looked to Grace. Arthur was still choking.

"Esperanza, we—"

"It's OK." Esperanza put a reassuring hand on Grace's shoulder. "It's really OK. I know why you're here. You think someone's been cheating to help Summerby win everything and you want to know who. If I were you, I'd be doing exactly the same."

Grace wasn't sure how to respond. How did Esperanza know so much?

"There have been a *lot* of suspicious wins by Summerby this year. *Greenfair's Got Talent* being one of them. And you don't believe it was a coincidence that both teams ended up using my mother as a choreographer."

Grace looked at Arthur and Kieran. She wasn't sure whether to nod or keep playing dumb. "I'm really sorry, though," Esperanza concluded before Grace could decide. "I don't think I'm going to be able to help. The bookings were made by each team captain."

Grace couldn't contain herself any longer. She could feel in her gut that they could trust Esperanza, and besides, she'd pretty much figured them out anyway.

"We spoke to the team captains," she blurted. "Summerby only booked it after Ms Morales returned their email ... which they never actually sent."

Esperanza frowned. "There *was* an email. But that wasn't sent by either of the team captains?"

"No!" Grace cried. They were so close to the

truth, she could feel it. If they could just see that email. "If we could just look at who sent—"

"I'm *really* sorry," Esperanza cut her off. "We delete all the emails once they're a month old."

Grace felt all her excitement burst. Esperanza's mum hadn't been fobbing them off with the "data protection" line after all. The information they needed really *was* gone. She, Arthur and Kieran looked at one another. Esperanza was their last hope – their very last lead ... What were they going to do now?

CHAPTER SIXTEEN

[Intro: Greenfair FM jingle (8 secs).]

GREENFAIR FM PRESENTERS TOGETHER: Good morning, Greenfair!

ROB: You're locked into Greenfair FM, Rob and Sinead with you on your Monday commute, it's just gone 8.03.

SINEAD: Still to come we've got news, travel and at 9 a.m., local author Helen Flam will be joining us for an exclusive interview about her new super-vegan cookbook, *The Year I Only Ate Peas*. Right up your street, eh, Rob?

ROB: Hmm, not sure about that, Sinead, but looking forward to hearing from Helen. And

right now, the moment you've all been waiting for ... We are thrilled to have selected the winner of our Park Protests Competition ...
SINEAD: We had entries from *ten* different schools in the local area and we've seen dozens of incredibly impressive young journalists. We watched your videos, listened to your demos, read your clippings ...
ROB: Man, there are a lot of talented kids out there!
SINEAD: There certainly are. But there can only be one winner to help us cover the Save Greenfair Park Protests, and that person is ...
TOGETHER: Michael Bernard of Summerby Secondary!

Arthur couldn't believe it. Well ... he *could* believe it. And yet he couldn't. Even though they'd hit so many brick walls while trying to figure out who was behind the Summerby fixes, he still had hope they would catch Michael. And now he realized they'd just been puppets and Michael had pulled all the strings. This was his aim all along. And he'd succeeded.

In a way, it felt satisfying to know the truth. But what good was the truth if you couldn't prove it, and broadcast it to the world? What good was the truth if you couldn't make a difference with it?

Arthur typed out a message to Grace and Kieran, and then to Anna. He knew how badly she wanted to win it as well. To make everything worse, Anna still hadn't spoken to him. He sat on his bed, twiddling his thumbs, waiting for the phone to buzz.

It buzzed. He leapt on it.

It was Grace, sending a row of fist-shaking emojis.

It buzzed again! He leapt on it.

It was Kieran, asking if he wanted to meet at the park.

It didn't buzz again.

Arthur buried his head in his hands. He really missed hanging out with Anna! He'd even listened to "Dads Heal in Time" for inspiration. (That was a new low.)

There was nothing to do but head out and meet Kieran. Arthur got there first and waited under the giant oak tree, and eventually Kieran popped up at the gates with his ball tucked under his arm. Even though they'd lost the competition, Michael was a cheat and they couldn't prove it, and Anna wasn't speaking to him, the sight of his best mate walking towards him through the park made everything seem a little sunnier.

"All right, mate." Kieran stood over him and dropped the ball on the ground. "I'm too gutted to talk about it. Shall we?"

What began as half-heartedly passing the ball back and forth quickly escalated into a fun, much-loved game of Hit My Hat, which basically just consisted of them trying to knock a hat off the other person's head without hitting them in the face. Arthur felt his worries lift as the high pressure target practice took his mind off his worries ... until Kieran made a *twenty metre* shot – his furthest yet – and kicked the ball *way* too close to Arthur's face.

Deciding that perhaps that was enough Hit My Hat for one day, the boys sat down under the tree. Everything Arthur had forgotten in the past half hour came crashing back. He glanced at his phone. Still no messages.

Kieran watched him. "So ... nothing from Anna?"

Arthur pouted. "Nope." Suddenly, he had a lightbulb moment. Maybe, instead of constantly lamenting how much better Kieran was with girls than him, he should actually ask him for some advice. Grace was always banging on about how her football team shared everything and how much it helped her with problems. He could at least *try* it.

"Actually, I was wondering if I, er, could . . ." What was happening? Arthur was fumbling over his words. With *Kieran*. Kieran who he had once seen eat a whole wheel of cheese in three bites, at his aunt's wedding, and then throw up in a plant pot. Arthur reminded himself that he had no reason to be nervous. But even though logically that was the case, and Kieran was his oldest friend, he was still a bit scared Kieran would laugh at him.

"What is it, mate?" Kieran encouraged.

"Can I talk to you about something?" Arthur squeaked.

"Oh, sure. What is it?"

Arthur coughed. "I wanted to ask your advice . . . about Anna."

"Oh? Well, it sounds like she's upset with you, mate." Kieran patted him on the shoulder.

"Well, yes, I got that. I'm not *that* dense."

Arthur bristled. "But . . . what do you think I should do?"

Kieran looked blankly at him for a moment. Arthur waited with baited breath for his wise words of counsel . . . and then, just as Arthur had feared, Kieran burst out guffawing.

Arthur started to blush. *This was so embarrassing.* He'd just totally gone to Kieran for help and now Kieran was laughing at him! *This was an actual nightmare.*

"It's all right for you, Kieran," he interrupted. "You talk to *loads* of girls. You just walk up to them and they're hanging off your every word. Say something in Spanish and they're all giggling like it's the funniest thing they've ever heard. But not all of us are so blessed . . ."

Kieran had stopped laughing by now. "Woah, Arthur, buddy," he said. "I wasn't laughing *at* you. I was laughing because you seem to think I know how to help!" He shrugged.

Arthur blinked. "Of course you know how to help," he said. "Girls love you."

"Yup." Kieran suddenly reached for the football lying beside them on the grass, and started twirling it around in his hands. "Girls love me . . . but, er, I'm not sure I love girls."

"*Oh*." Out of all the things he had guessed Kieran might say, this wasn't one of them. "So you mean . . ."

Kieran passed the football from hand to hand, still not looking at Arthur. "I'm not sure," he replied after a moment. "I'm not sure who I like. Or if I like anyone."

"Oh," Arthur said again, as he tried to process what Kieran was saying. Kieran had always seemed so sure of himself before.

"You see, my friend, I'm even more confused than you are," Kieran went on. He finally stopped playing with the ball and grinned at Arthur.

"So it would seem." Arthur grinned back.

"We're just a couple of doughnuts," Kieran said. "Super-confused doughnuts."

Arthur nodded. He didn't have any more idea about what to do than when he started the conversation. But he felt better. It felt good knowing that someone who seemed as "sorted" as Kieran was just as clueless as he was. He thought to himself, yet again, that the more he got to know people, the more he realized everyone had their own things going on – things that you might not expect. He remembered getting to know Grace properly for the first time and realizing that she was actually embarrassed about her Nigerian heritage.

He leaned back against the tree, breathing a sigh of relief.

"So, I don't know if this will help or not, but in movies you always see people making, like, *grand gestures* for each other, don't you?" Kieran suggested. "You could, like, I don't know . . .

get your dad to help write her a song? Serenade her on *Radio Royalty?*"

Arthur wrinkled his nose. That sounded *mortifying.* Kieran glimpsed the look on Arthur's face. "Nah, it sounded stupid even as I was saying it," he said. "I don't know, this isn't advice about girls, really, just people in general. But . . . have you actually said sorry?"

Arthur sat bolt upright. "No," he croaked. "Agh!" He hit his palm to his forehead. *Duh!* How could he have missed the most simple solution in the entire world?

Kieran shook his head. "You doughnut, Arthur."

Arthur *was* a doughnut. The biggest, doughiest doughnut ever to walk the planet. Covered in icing and extra sprinkles. All this time he'd been thinking of Anna like she was some alien species, when all anyone in the world ever wanted to hear was an apology when someone has upset them!

"She'll be at the protests tomorrow, right?" Kieran said.

Arthur nodded.

"So you'll find her then." Kieran patted Arthur on the back and Arthur shook his head one last time at his own silliness. Just *say* sorry. *Simple!*

"I still can't *believe* Michael got away with cheating, and we never got our fair chance to help cover the protests." Kieran finally let himself voice his disappointment. "Even though it seemed unlikely, there was a little part of me that thought interviewing Esperanza would lead to a breakthrough."

"I know," Arthur agreed. He'd felt the same. Somehow, even though it seemed impossible, he'd *desperately* hoped they'd crack the case.

They looked around their beloved park. "Michael *is* a cheat," Kieran said thoughtfully, "but ... we've read enough of his work to know that at least he'll do a good job covering the protests."

Arthur nodded. Now that the protests were approaching, bringing Michael down seemed less and less important. As long as *someone* was telling their story to the nation, then that was the most important thing. Tomorrow they'd *all* be there to fight for their park, whether they were the ones on air or not.

He and Kieran both looked around the park for a moment. Some little kids were feeding the ducks and some others were climbing trees. One boy fell off and landed on his bum, laughing. It hit Arthur that the protests were really *tomorrow*. The threat of losing all this seemed more real than ever. What would they do if the protests didn't work?

CHAPTER
SEVENTEEN

[Intro: Greenfair FM jingle (8 secs).]

MICHAEL: Hello, people of Greenfair. You're live with Greenfair FM as the, er, angry mobs file in to protest the stunning new flats in the town of Greenfair, which will help improve the area and grow the economy, as well as meeting a desperate accommodation shortage. Oh, it looks like the crowds are getting out of control as one of the protesters has just thrown a small child's ice cream on to the floor . . .

The day of the protests had finally arrived. Michael had been set up with a deck, with the familiar *GREENFAIR FM 96.3* logo emblazoned on a banner behind him. There were two giant speakers transmitting his voice across the park, as well as to listeners at home. In between speaking, Michael was putting out live updates on the *Greenfair Weekly* website. There were a few other local journalists and someone from *Greenfair FM* accompanying him, but it seemed like Michael was the main coverage of the event. Arthur couldn't lie to himself . . . He was crazy jealous, and livid that Michael had got there through cheating. But he tried to focus on the bigger picture. Even if he wasn't helping to publicize the protests, Michael was.

Or, was he?

Arthur scratched his head as he listened to Michael's reporting. What *was* he talking about? Looking to one side at the protester Michael had been referring to, Arthur saw that it was a young man with a placard, who had seen a child drop her ice-cream and was now helping to clear it up because the dad had his hands full. Arthur blinked, looking around for the scene that Michael was describing.

Could it be described as an "angry mob"? The protesters seemed pretty peaceful to him. Everyone was just standing around in the sunshine waving their placards. Occasionally a chant of "SAVE GREENFAIR" would start up. The energy in the air felt intense, electric and impassioned – Arthur could feel how much everyone desperately wanted to save the park, but it didn't feel hostile. Where had Michael got that from?

Everyone had shown up. Arthur could see Mr P and his husband with a sign that said "I SPEAK FOR THE TREES." Esperanza and her mother were holding hands and waving their arms in the air. Ms Lyall, Roddy and Roddy's younger brother, Benjy, were wearing SAVE OUR PARK T-shirts. When Benjy saw Arthur he gave him a small wave. Summerby had turned out in full force, too. Arthur saw Ms Lyall and the Summerby head teacher give each other a curt nod. They were just as competitive as the students, thought Arthur with a smile. Tilly-Mae and all the Summerby football squad were there, hanging out with Lia. Diaz and the rest of FemSoc were clapping and trying to keep a chant going.

Arthur spied Grace and Kieran waving at him from the other side of

the park and headed over to greet them.

Grace swept her arm out, gesturing to the crowds. "There are *so* many people! The energy is amazing!"

"It feels like we might actually save the park!" Kieran added. "Except ... Have you heard Michael?"

Grace, Arthur and Kieran all listened closely. Michael was still talking about the "accommodation shortage" and how important it was to build more places for people to live.

"Duh! How wrong can you be!" shouted Grace.

Kieran was still listening. "I don't know, he's

pretty convincing, he's making it sound like . . .
the development is a *good* thing?"

"But what he's saying isn't accurate," said
Grace. "According to what Esperanza was
telling us, it's important to build more *affordable*
living for people. Not luxury flats for the elite."

"What is Michael doing?" Arthur agreed. "I
thought every kid in the area wanted to keep
Greenfair Park."

They all stared at Michael, who was avoiding
eye contact with anyone in the crowd. He was
usually quite self-assured – quiet and business-
like, yes, but confident – except, today he
seemed meek and reticent. Almost like *he*
didn't even believe what he was saying. The
crowds were starting to pick up on it, too. With
hardly any other media here, Michael's voice
was the only one being heard. Grace, Arthur
and Kieran looked around and saw frowns and
shrugs. A murmur of confusion rippled through

the crowd.

Then Arthur spied Anna by the other side of the park, under the giant oak tree. He gulped and felt for the card in his pocket. It contained an apology and a Snickers. Arthur worried that he might stumble over his words if he tried to apologize verbally, so he figured it was better to write it down.

Kieran patted him on the shoulder. "Godspeed," he said solemnly.

Arthur gulped again.

As he approached Anna, he saw she was standing amongst a giant group of mates. As he came close they all seemed to scowl at him and whisper. Was there any sight more terrifying than an angry flock of girls? It was like they sensed that he'd upset Anna and they were closing in around her, turning their backs on him like frosty, supportive penguins.

He reached forward to tap Anna on the

shoulder. "Can we, er . . ." he tried to ignore the icy glares of her friends, "chat?"

Anna nodded and extricated herself from the huddle. Stepping behind the big oak tree, there was a moment of properly awkward silence.

Arthur reached inside his pocket and held out the card. "I got you something." His heart was thumping double-time.

Anna accepted and opened it. Arthur looked away and held his breath, waiting for her reaction.

"Er . . . Arthur," she said.

Was she going to throw the Snickers back in his face? Had her chocolate preferences changed since they last spoke? Maybe she was into Mars bars, now? What if she didn't even want his apology? What if it was too late?

"Yes?" he squeaked.

"I can't read it. It's, er, well, it's a bit melted." She turned the card round. His carefully thought-out message, that he spent hours crafting and then rewriting over and over until his handwriting looked neat enough, was *covered* in thick, gooey milk chocolate. You could barely make out his writing from under the smears. Just the word "sorry".

They both looked at the card for a second, then at each other, then burst out laughing. Really, really laughing. Achy-belly-hurt laughing. Rolling around on the floor laughing.

"Your face," Anna wheezed. "What is it . . . that Kieran . . . always calls you?"

"A doughnut," Arthur laughed.

"Yup." Anna took several breaths to recover. "Solid gold *doughnut*."

"I'm sorry," Arthur said finally.

"I'm sorry too." Anna shook her head. "I *was* annoyed, but I know how it looked with the notebook. Plus, you know how I never actually told you who I was the first time I met you? It was because I was nervous. Stupid, really."

Arthur felt heat rising in his cheeks. *She* was nervous around *him?*

"I should have replied to you sooner," Anna went on. "I was ... well, I was embarrassed that you knew I'd been taking notes from our conversations, about radio tips and stuff."

Arthur blinked. "Why would you be embarrassed about that?"

"I guess I've been worrying ..." Anna took a deep breath. "That you're better than me."

Arthur's eyes widened. Was Anna kidding? "No way!" he cried. "I've been worrying that *you're* better than *me.*"

Anna snorted. "Shut up."

"No, really." Arthur ran a hand through his

hair. "You're so, like, quick and funny and . . ." His cheeks turned red. Was he actually saying these things out loud?

Anna smiled shyly. "I guess we're both doughnuts."

Arthur nodded. They'd both got things so mixed up! Anna reached forward and gave him a hug. Arthur inhaled the smell of coconut mixed with lemons then stopped himself before she heard him sniffing like a weirdo.

"I've been feeling so nervous that I didn't even submit for the Park Protests Competition in the end," Anna said, pulling away.

"What?!" Arthur's eyes bugged out of his head.

"I panicked that, because my style is funny, they'd be looking for something more serious. Plus, I got worried that I'd been taking so many notes from you, Grace, and Michael, I should step aside . . ."

Arthur felt gutted for her. "*Everyone* has

something to learn from other people. I bet even . . . the Dalai Lama."

Anna snort-laughed. "I know. I regretted it after. I'll never let my nerves get in the way of going for something that I want, ever again."

Arthur thought to himself, once again, how different people were once you got to know them. When she was presenting, Anna seemed like the most confident person on the planet.

"With you backing out, and with all the manufactured Victory Road losses, it's no wonder Michael won . . ." Arthur shook his head.

"And now he's making the protests sound like a bad thing!" Anna added. "But I don't get why? What is *up* with him?"

Arthur furrowed his brow. "I don't know. But right now, that doesn't matter. We just need to make him stop."

"Let's find the others." Anna nodded.

***

While Arthur was gone, Grace had been plotting. She'd tried *so hard* to see the positives in Michael covering these protests. OK, so, he got there by cheating, but she figured that the most important thing was that *someone* was doing Greenfair Park justice.

But Michael wasn't. He wasn't even giving it a chance. He was making it sound like the park didn't matter. She thought of all her own memories in this place, of *everyone's* memories – of all the people who had spent time here walking their dogs, kicking balls around, delicately weaving daisy chains, of how all these people had shown up to save it and Michael was making it sound like no one would care if it was gone. It was false reporting, fake news! She'd thought that his motive had been simply to win, but now she wondered what else was going on.

Grace thought of Esperanza and how she'd managed to make actual change in the world, and felt all her determination rise up again in a hot, fierce bubble. She wouldn't give up yet. She might not be on Greenfair FM, but she still had a voice.

When Arthur returned with Anna, Grace pounced. "We need to—"

"—Do something," Arthur finished.

"If only we could prove that Michael cheated," said Kieran. "Then surely he'd get taken off air, and someone else could cover the protests truthfully?"

"How can we prove it, though?" Arthur frantically ran his hands through his hair. "Esperanza said the email was gone. We're out of ideas!"

"Email?" Anna asked. "What email?"

"We think that Michael was the one to

book the same choreographer for both teams, knowing they'd do the same routine," Arthur explained. "We spoke to Esperanza who takes the bookings, and she said all the emails have been deleted."

Anna bit her lip thoughtfully. "I think . . ."

They all turned to look at her.

"I think I know someone who *might* be able to help."

CHAPTER EIGHTEEN

[Intro: *Best of the Best* jingle (7 secs).]

GRACE: Welcome to *Best of the Best's* Tech Troubles, where our topic of the day is HACKING. And no, this isn't a guide for would-be cyber criminals, we're *of course* talking about how to protect yourself and your tech. But that does mean getting inside the minds of the hackers themselves so that you're always one step ahead. So, here we have a handy guide ...

Step one: learn a programming language. Side note — if you're a serious hacker, then you'd probably learn more than one. But remember,

```
learning a language takes time, so be patient
with yourself ...
Step two: Secure your machine ...
```

"Tilly-Mae, I had no idea you were such a computer genius ..." Grace added.

"Yeah, well, if you admit you can fix computers you tend to find yourself with a lot of *friends*. Especially when they've got computer problems. That's what my dad says, anyway." Tilly-Mae shrugged. "So I mostly keep it to myself."

"Gotcha," Grace said. "So, Tilly-Mae ..."

"And if you're a hairdresser. A *lot* of friends who want free haircuts. Some jobs are just like that, you know? But hacking can be done in secret. Hairdressing, not so much."

"Do you like hairdressing?" Grace asked.

"God no, why?" Tilly-Mae answered, as if

it was a really strange question. Lia wasn't here to translate, so Grace looked at Arthur, Kieran and Anna. They all shrugged.

"When did you get into computers?" Grace moved on.

"I never really got into it. I was more ... born into it, I guess. My mum and my dad both work in IT. You know how some kids are bi-lingual because their parents are fluent in French or whatever? That's kind of like me, with Python."

"Uh-huh, interesting," Grace said, although she had zero idea what a snake had to do with it. She peered over her shoulder. "And after a lengthy, tense few minutes of frantic typing, we're into the server ... Tilly-Mae, can you talk me through what you're doing now?"

Tilly-Mae side-eyed Grace, as if to say, *No, please be quiet*. Clearly, she now needed to concentrate. Grace reluctantly lowered her microphone and tried to wait patiently while Tilly–Mae continued typing. This was taking too long. What if the protests finished before they managed to retrieve the email? What if retrieving the email wasn't possible? Grace tried not to let herself think about that.

They'd looked for Esperanza, to ask for access to her email account to try to retrieve the deleted emails. Weirdly, though, when they'd seen Esperanza she'd glanced in their direction and shuffled quickly away. Grace guessed that she must have been super busy, so they ended up ringing Esperanza's mother Sofia and asking her instead. She'd been reluctant at first, but when they told her it could play a part in helping to save Greenfair, she'd given them the password. After all, she wanted to save the park too – possibly even more than they did.

"Et, voila!" called Tilly–Mae, at last. "I'm making progress!"

Kieran, Grace, Anna and Arthur silently cheered. They were fizzing with nervous, excited energy.

It had taken some convincing to get Tilly-Mae to agree to do this. Her motto (which she'd told them all proudly) was "just cause you've got the skills, don't do it for the thrills." She considered herself an "ethical hacker". But once they explained why they were doing it, and that it could be key to saving Greenfair, Tilly-Mae was more than willing to help. She'd brandished a laptop from within her bag, which she always carried on her "just in case".

"I'll give it my best shot," she'd said. "But time is tight."

Now it seemed like they were in luck. Maybe.

"Don't get too excited just because I'm in the server," Tilly-Mae said. "Searching for deleted emails, ones that have been removed from the recycle bin, is a whole different kettle of bees.

Especially if they've been gone for more than thirty days."

They all nodded. None of them fully understood what Tilly-Mae was doing, but they did understand that finding what they were looking for was going to be a challenge, even though they were so close.

"OK ... I'm going in." Tilly-Mae had a *serious business* face on.

They waited for a few more painstaking minutes, staring intensely at Tilly-Mae, who was staring intensely at the screen. Every now and then Tilly-Mae would mutter something undecipherable under her breath, or say "ooh" or "aah" in a way that could be excited or frustrated.

"Is that good or bad? Good or bad?" Kieran whispered.

Arthur shrugged in response, just as confused and on edge as Kieran was. Grace had bitten her fingernails down.

After what felt like *for ever*, Tilly-Mae took a deep breath and shut the laptop lid. Grace, Arthur and Kieran practically fell on top of her.

"Well?"

"Did you find anything?"

"Were you able to locate it?" They all started talking at the same time.

Tilly-Mae looked up at them, and in that moment they knew it was over. She gave a defeated whistle and a slow, regretful shake of her head. "I'm really sorry, guys," she said. "I can't find anything at all relating to Summerby or Victory Road in the deleted-deleted items. Not a sausage."

The disappointment was crushing. They all felt their last, rekindled hopes whoosh out of them.

"You're sure?" said Arthur softly.

"Positive, sorry." Tilly-Mae really did look as disappointed as they felt.

They all sat down on the grass. Grace couldn't look anyone in the eye, and she couldn't look at the park either. It was too painful. So she just looked at her hands. Tilly-Mae started putting her laptop away.

"Unless . . ." said Arthur.

Grace and Kieran looked up. Tilly-Mae stopped packing her computer in her bag.

"No, it's stupid," Arthur said.

"What? Any ideas welcome at this point, mate," Kieran said.

"Well . . . I don't know. I'm just wondering if we're overthinking this. Esperanza never said the email had been deleted from her deleted items. She just said it had been deleted. Have we checked the recycle bin?"

Tilly-Mae blinked. "I assumed she'd already looked there. If it was just in the recycle bin, surely she'd have found it for you?"

Arthur shrugged. "I don't know. I'm

just thinking of my dad when it comes to computers. He's a bit of a doughnut. Like, he'll say he's lost a document when he's just closed the tab or something."

"Esperanza is seventeen, not fifty," Tilly-Mae replied.

"But it's worth a shot?" Arthur knew it was desperate, but now he'd thought it, they had to check. He'd never forgive himself if they messed up the whole investigation over something so simple.

Tilly-Mae rolled her eyes and opened her laptop again. "OK, well, let's disregard the last ten minutes of *supreme* technological skill, shall we, and just *look in the recycle bi*—" Suddenly, she stopped talking. Her mouth fell open.

Arthur's breath caught in his throat. "Is it there?!" He could barely contain himself. "Is it in the recycle bin?"

Tilly-Mae frowned. "No . . ." she said. But

there was a slight glint in her eye. "It was in the inbox."

Everyone fell silent. Kieran wrinkled his nose like there was a bad smell under it. "In the *inbox?*" Kieran repeated.

Tilly-Mae nodded. "It was there all along. Not deleted at all. Take a look for yourselves."

The trio scrambled over Tilly-Mae's shoulder at once, desperate to get a look at the screen. The email read:

Dear Danza Studios,

I'm writing to enquire after your services. Our school's dance team, *Strictly Summerby*, is looking for a choreographer and we've heard of your excellent reputation. Please call us on this number. We look forward to hearing from you soon.

Then there was a telephone number and no sign off name. The email *sounded* like Michael, exactly like him in fact. He was the only kid they knew who could sound like a middle-aged businessman. But there was no name on the email!

"What's the email address?!" Grace squinted.

"M.Stow," Tilly-Mae read.

"*Stow*," Kieran repeated. "What's Michael's last name?"

"Bernard," Arthur answered.

The five of them looked at each other in confusion. "Stow?" Kieran repeated. "Are there any Stows at your school?" He looked at Tilly-Mae and Anna, who shook their heads.

"Argh!" Arthur couldn't help but want to tear his hair out. "We take one step forward in this investigation and three steps back!"

"Not quite." Grace raised her hand. "We know one thing for certain."

The others looked at her. Grace couldn't believe what she was about to say, but the evidence was staring her right in the face.

"Esperanza lied to us. The email was sitting in her inbox all along. She's got something to hide."

Arthur put a hand on Grace's shoulder. He knew how much she'd looked up to Esperanza, and this new information was a blow. They all thought Esperanza had been on their side . . .

"You're right," Arthur said. "I hate to say it, but Esperanza is our new lead."

CHAPTER NINETEEN

[Intro: *Radio Royalty: This Is Your Life* instrumental (6 secs)]

ARTHUR: Hello and welcome to Radio Royalty's *This is Your Life: the Greenfair Park edition*. Today I'm out and about in the neighbourhood with residents of our local community as they share their favourite memories of Greenfair Park. With me right now is Mr Gupta of Appleby Road. Mr Gupta, am I right in saying you've lived in this area for sixty years?

MR GUPTA: That's right ...

ARTHUR: So, what's your most treasured memory of our much-loved park?

MR GUPTA: *Laughs* Oh, well, there is one

incident that really sticks in my mind
involving my daughter, an excitable shitzu,
several sausages, and a game of extreme
frisbee ...]

With no time to lose, Grace, Kieran, Arthur and Anna had thanked Tilly-Mae and set off into the crowd. They needed to find Esperanza, but they had to be subtle about it because if she saw them looking for her then she'd surely bolt for it again. She was obviously avoiding them. So, they had decided to employ their usual tactic of pretending to interview people about the park, and then maybe they'd track her down.

When Michael had won the competition, they hadn't even bothered attempting to cover the event themselves, because they'd assumed everyone would tune into Greenfair FM. But interviewing and chatting to so many different people about the park, how they used it and what they loved about it, was turning out to be an uplifting and moving experience, whether or not anyone was listening.

"So what's *your* favourite memory of Greenfair Park?" Arthur asked one woman. She was there with her two small children, one in a pram and one standing beside her, tugging at her hand.

She gestured to her older child. "This one took their first steps right over there."

"Oh wow!" Kieran said. "A proper big moment!"

"It was," the woman beamed. "They love toddling about here. We come here most days.

I don't know where I'd take them otherwise. There's the soft play but it's just not the same as being outdoors, is it?"

Arthur shook his head. No, it wasn't.

"My girlfriend and I met here, and we used to come here for dates," said one man. "We were just teenagers, then. We used to lie in the grass and look up at the stars and talk about the future. We're married now. Twenty years." He showed them his wedding ring. Arthur, Kieran, Grace and Anna all peered over at the ring. They could barely imagine knowing someone for that long. And it all started in this park!

"We live just over there." He pointed to the row of houses just behind the park. "We still come here for a late night stroll, now and again. It's funny to think that this place may not be here any more. It just wouldn't seem like home."

"We LOVE it here!" said one young girl. "This is the best park ever! The trees are so good for climbing. There's one branch on that tree" – she pointed at a large oak – "that fits my bum perfectly. I sit and read in it."

Her friend started giggling wildly. Arthur, Kieran, Anna and Grace smiled at the "bum-shaped" branch in question.

"It's true, though," the first girl went on. "Where am I going to find another tree like that? It's *freakish*. It's like it grew just for me and my bum."

"What do you read up there?" Grace asked.

"At the moment I'm reading *Chronicles of Narnia*," she said. "Reading outside is so different to reading indoors. I look up through the branches of the tree and it's like I'm *in* Narnia."

Grace nodded. Reading here in the park on a lazy, summer day was one of her favourite things to do too.

"We've got pretty good at climbing, too," said her friend. "A few weeks ago we nearly reached the top branch."

The group looked up towards the sky. It was a *big* tree.

"That's impressive," Kieran commented.

"Not as impressive as when I reach the *top*," the girl said. "I mean, unless they cut it down before I get there." Her eyes suddenly filled with sadness, as if the threat to the park was becoming real to her for the very first time.

They talked to all sorts of people. From people who were new to the area to people who had lived here longer than they'd been alive, from young kids to grandparents. Everyone had their own reasons for loving the park but everyone was unified in how much they wanted to save it. It was so absorbing that it was hard not to be distracted from their ultimate goal of finding Esperanza.

"How could anyone say that a block of luxury flats is worth more than all this?" Anna asked in wonder.

"It's unbelievable," Grace agreed. Her mind was boggling.

Unfortunately, Michael's coverage seemed to be taking effect. Along the way they could hear some people becoming genuinely confused as to whether they were protesting for a good cause, with whispers like, "Do you think he's right? Are the flats really going to bring in more jobs?"

Not everybody, though. Some people were clearly outraged by Michael's words, shaking their fists and booing, and then others – like Mr P and many of the other Victory Roaders – were still in high spirits. But while they remained firm in their opinion and resolve, Grace could feel the energy of the protest ebbing away. "What's the point being here, if the information is getting spun like this?" people were saying. Surely it was only a matter of time before people started tailing off, Grace thought, biting her nails.

She clung on to the desperate hope they could still prove Michael cheated and stop his broadcast, but they were *still* no closer to finding Esperanza. As Arthur's eyes scoured the park for her, they landed on something else.

"Guys." Arthur put his hand out to halt the group.

"What? Is it Esperanza?" Grace asked.

Arthur shook his head. "Look at that poster."

The group turned. On the park gates was a giant poster, with a floor plan and layout of the proposed flats.

"What is it?" Kieran squinted at the poster.

"Look at the name," said Arthur.

"Stow Developments," Anna read aloud. As

soon as she did, all three of them swung around to look at Arthur.

"*Stow*," Grace repeated. "As in, M.Stow? The person who sent the email to Esperanza's mum?"

"*No way.*" Anna shook her head.

"This *cannot* be a coincidence," Grace added.

"What does this mean?" Kieran shouted.

"I'm not sure yet ..." Arthur said. "But I think I might have a hunch."

All kinds of dots were joining up in his head. He pulled his phone out and played his interview with Diaz, months ago.

"So Michael's your best mate, right? How long have you known him?" Arthur's voice rang out.

"We used to live on the same street. That was before Michael moved in with his mum and changed his name and stuff ..." Diaz's voice answered.

The group stared at Arthur. He played it again, *". . . and changed his name and stuff . . ."* Diaz's voice rang out. *"Changed his name."*

"Anna, do you remember Michael changing his name?" Grace asked.

"No." Anna shook her head. "Michael's last name has been Bernard ever since he joined Summerby. I'm positive."

"How much do you want to bet . . ." Arthur started.

"That Michael's name used to be Stow?" said a voice from behind them.

CHAPTER TWENTY

```
[Intro: Radio Royalty, Your Family Tree jingle
(4 secs.)]
KIERAN: Hello and welcome to Your Family Tree,
where we find routes to your roots. Today we
learn that Michael Bernard is descended from
a long line of property developers ...
```

The group, who had been hunched over Arthur's phone, turned to find Esperanza behind them. She was holding a bunch of papers in her right hand and she looked absolutely *fuming*.

"You'd be right," Esperanza said. She shook

the papers. "One Michael Stow became Michael Bernard after his parents' divorce. He is the *nephew* of the owner of Stow Developments, the company planning to build this new block of luxury flats and destroy our park with no regard for the community, environment or anyone else but themselves."

Arthur, Grace, Kieran and Anna stared at Esperanza open-mouthed. It was a lot to process, but it made a huge amount of sense.

"Are you sure?" Grace asked.

"Yes." Esperanza put the newspaper down in front of them. It was an old one, dated a few years back, with a headline: "STOW DEVELOPMENTS OPEN LUXURY FLATS IN THE TOWN OF GRUNDLEWOOD." Underneath was a picture of an older guy cutting a ribbon in front of a new, shiny apartment block, accompanied by a man and a woman who they assumed were Michael's parents, and a small boy. He was much younger, but it was unmistakably Michael.

"But that's . . . corrupt! They can't do this!" Grace cried, staring aghast at the picture. "The property developers' nephew can't go on live radio to tell the town what a good thing the flats are! He's obviously biased! If everyone *knew* that . . ."

"Then they'd know the coverage was propaganda?" Esperanza folded her arms.

"Exactly!" Grace felt like she might burst into tears at the injustice of it all.

"How much do you want to bet they arranged that no one else was covering this event, too?" Esperanza went on. "Where do you think all the other press are? Hmm? Every single journalist here is a Stow Developments buddy," she spat.

The group were shocked. Could journalism really be twisted in this way? All of this "fake news" talk they'd heard from their parents was starting to make sense.

But Grace was still confused. She'd looked up to Esperanza, and Esperanza had let them down. If she'd shown them the email instead of lying about it, they might have been able to put two and two together sooner and stop Michael. Now, he'd won the competition and spent all morning making Stow Developments' plans sound amazing.

"Why did you lie to us?" she cried. All journalistic professionalism was out the window and Grace couldn't help showing how upset she was.

Esperanza fiddled with her bracelet. Her long, dark hair fell in front of her face. "I'm sorry," she said quietly. "I lied because ... I helped Michael plan the Double Dance Disaster."

Everyone fell silent. Despite the protests going on in the background, the air around them was so quiet you could hear a pin drop.

"I knew that my mum was accidentally teaching the same routine to two different groups for the same event and . . . I said nothing. I knew it was a disaster waiting to happen and I just let it carry on."

Grace looked at the others. Everyone seemed completely puzzled by Esperanza's confession.

"But *why?*" Grace asked.

"You might have guessed when we spoke before, but, my mum's business isn't exactly thriving." Esperanza coughed awkwardly. "She's so good at what she does and it's her passion, but it's tough. When I realized the bookings were a conflict of interest it did confuse me, so I looked into it further and learned Michael's identity. I confronted him about it, and he said he'd pay us extra if I said nothing. Mum was going to get paid double for the booking and I didn't feel like we could afford to say no ... When you came in, I knew

260

the Double Dance Disaster must have been part of something bigger, but I was afraid that if I showed you the email I'd get found out, and . . . I was ashamed."

Despite herself, Grace felt her heart break a little for Esperanza. She could understand wanting to protect your family like that.

"It *was* part of something bigger," Arthur said. "Michael's been plotting Victory Road's downfall for months, so we wouldn't beat him in the Park Protests competition and *he'd* be the one to cover it."

Esperanza looked crestfallen. "And now I've helped Stow Developments essentially take down my mother's business for good. How's that for karma?" She gave a hollow laugh.

No one knew what to say. Even though she had made a mistake, they didn't feel like rubbing salt in the wound. Esperanza looked like she had punished herself enough.

"But now we know the truth," Arthur suggested tentatively, "and we have actual *proof* that Michael cheated to win, we can stop the broadcast, surely? And once everyone knows that he's related to Stow Developments, no one will take what he's been saying seriously . . ."

"I'm sorry to break it to you . . ." Esperanza sounded choked up. "But my friend's mum works at the council, and she told me they are right this moment signing off the final agreement for the flats. It's too late."

"WHAT?" Anna shouted.

"Clearly they weren't convinced by the protests or the amount of support for the park." Esperanza sounded like she might cry. "The flats are going to be built."

"No!" Grace cried. "No, surely not? There must be some way we can use what we know. This is corrupt!"

Grace couldn't believe it. Having come so

far, it couldn't possibly be *too late*?

Esperanza shrugged. "At this point, the only thing that could save the park would be if the flat developments were literally illegal in some way, like ... if there were protected species living here. I ran home earlier to do some research ..." She moved the newspaper, revealing a bunch of other printed sheets of wildlife. "... but I don't really know what I'm looking for. And no one cares about ducks or tadpoles or water-snails or newts!"

Grace picked up the sheets of endangered animals. Esperanza had put a cross through every one, meaning none of them had ever been recorded in the Greenfair Park pond. She looked at the picture of a great crested newt, which was on the protected list, and thought of the newts Anna had been talking about in her wildlife segment. It was so sad those little guys were going to lose their homes, even if they weren't endangered. They looked pretty similar to the great crested newts, only it said on the sheet these were usually a lot larger than other newts, around seventeen centimetres.

Suddenly, Grace's eyes widened. "Anna, how big was the newt in your Wildlife Weekly segment?"

"Um, I can't remember," Anna answered.

Grace got out her phone and skipped back to her recording of her interview with Anna.

"Classic grey-brown, with an orange belly and black spots all over, but he's a big one, though! About fifteen centimetres. They're usually only ten," Anna's voice sounded.

The others all stopped and listened.

"They're usually only ten centimetres." Grace played the clip again. She looked at the sheet, and then at the pond.

"Guys," she said, hardly daring to hope. "What if we *did* have an endangered species living in this pond? What would that mean?"

"I'm not exactly sure. But I know it would cause complications."

Grace's heart started beating double-time. "Anna!" she said breathlessly. "Anna, did you take any pictures of the newt you included in your wildlife segment?"

"Um, yeah, I think so." Anna got her phone out. She scrolled back through. Everyone crowded round, trying to get a look.

Grace held the picture up to compare to the endangered great crested newt. "You said smooth newts are usually only ten centimetres, and this one was fifteen."

Everyone squinted at the two pictures of the newts, starting to process what Grace was saying.

"Grace, if you're right ..." Esperanza breathed. "Then this could blow the whole thing wide open."

CHAPTER TWENTY-ONE

[Intro: Greenfair FM News jingle (8 secs).]

GREENFAIR FM NEWS PRESENTER: And now, for a breaking news bulletin from our Park Protests correspondent, we cross back to Michael Bernard live in Greenfair Park ...

MICHAEL: Uh, this, um, just in ... The council have approved the final plans for the flats ... Looks like, uh, today's protests have been fruitless ...

Grace could barely breathe. She didn't dare to hope that they might yet save Greenfair

Park. Not after everything else they'd been through.

The thing was, they couldn't take this directly to Stow Developments and trust they would do the right thing. Instead, they needed to make their new knowledge public somehow. Plus, they still weren't sure if the newt was a great crested newt or not and, if it was, what that would actually mean. They weren't animal experts, or lawyers . . . But they *did* know where they could find some.

As soon as it hit them that the smooth newt Anna had found could *in fact* possibly be an endangered, great crested newt, Arthur had taken off at speed to get his mum. She was a lawyer, and could tell them exactly what this meant. Meanwhile Anna had taken off in the opposite direction to find her sister, who was an Environmental Conservation Education and Engagement Officer ... in other words, a wildlife expert.

But in the meantime, Michael had just announced to the world that the development would be going ahead.

As soon as he'd said it, there was a collective gasp followed by silence across the park. Even Michael sounded down about the news, Grace thought to herself in bafflement. But she supposed she must be misinterpreting that – after all, he was helping to destroy the park!

People all around them had put down their placards. Michael had stopped broadcasting and the Greenfair FM team were beginning to pack up. Everyone was ready to leave, and an air of gloom had settled.

It's not over, Grace told herself, but she knew they were running out of time. If Arthur and his mum, and Anna and her sister, came back to an empty park, then how would they tell everyone about their discovery?

"We need to stall," Esperanza said. "If only we had some way to do our own broadcast."

"We could do it on *Listen Up!*" Grace said. "But it's only school radio and no one would be tuned into it. Everyone's tuned into Greenfair FM. How are we going to get people to listen to us instead?"

Esperanza rubbed her forehead. She didn't know. On some level, Grace had been secretly hoping that this impressive older girl who she admired so much would make a miracle happen. That she would take matters into her own hands and sort everything out. But even someone like Esperanza didn't have *all* the answers all the time. Grace closed her eyes and tried to think hard. There must be something they could do . . .

Then she opened her eyes. She watched Anna dashing through the crowd, determined to find her sister. Grace had thought the worst of Anna and had never thought they'd work on the same side, but they wouldn't have spotted the possible endangered species if it wasn't for her. Grace looked across at Lia and Tilly-Mae. They were leaving the park looking sad, but they had their arms around each other in support. She had doubted them, too, but they'd both turned out to be instrumental in the investigation. They never would have found that email if it wasn't for Tilly-Mae. There were so many discoveries they wouldn't have made if they *hadn't* worked with Summerby instead of against them.

Looking around her now, all Grace could see were students from Victory Road and students from Summerby Secondary who all wanted the same thing. She had one, last idea. But if that didn't work then it really was game over.

***

"Psst, Michael," Grace hissed.

Michael's expression was one of alarm when he noticed Grace, as if he thought she might throw a water balloon at him. But nonetheless he approached her cautiously.

"What is it, Grace?" he asked. He seemed *sad*. Like, *properly* sad. Once again, Grace couldn't help wondering why. He'd won. He'd dominated the airwaves with his own opinion and helped his family.

"We know your uncle owns Stow Developments," Grace said.

Michael looked down at his shoes and didn't say anything.

"We know you've been cheating so that you could win this competition, so you could help your family business. I get wanting to do anything for your family, I do, but other people have families that are going to be affected by this, too. All we're asking for is a chance for both sides of the story to be heard."

Grace prayed that appealing to Michael's inner journalist would be enough. Before this happened, she was sure he wanted to make sure people's voices were heard as much as she did. Maybe he just needed to be reminded.

Michael looked up. "Are you going to tell the whole world I cheated?" he asked.

Grace had to admit that blackmail had crossed her mind. If she threatened to tell Summerby and Victory Road what Michael had done, every kid in a three-mile radius would turn on him.

"No," Grace said. "I'm just going to ask you to help us, like a real, fair journalist would. I know you don't care about the park, but . . ."

"I do!" Michael shouted. "I do care about the park! Of course I do!"

Grace didn't know how to respond. If he cared about the park, then what was he doing?

Michael pointed to the left side of the park. "I learned how to ride a bike right over there, before my mum and dad split up. My birthday before last, we had a family picnic right under that tree. I love this place."

Michael *loved* this place? So why had he spent the entire day acting like he didn't care if it was paved over? "Then why did . . .?" Grace started.

"My uncle has been really good to me and my mum since my dad left," Michael sniffed. "It's been hard on us. We had to leave our house and move in with him for a while. I don't know what we would have done if he hadn't been there. He was the one who suggested this whole thing. He's been helping me."

"How?" Grace asked.

Michael looked pained but relieved at the same time, like he was finally getting something off his chest that had been weighing on him.

"He asked me to listen in on conversations. Like, on the bus, I overheard Arthur telling Anna about what Victory Road were planning, so I sent the team captain an anonymous tip . . ."

Grace felt so guilty for ever thinking it was Anna. She couldn't believe Michael had been getting away with this for so long.

"And he taught me how to hack," Michael carried on. "That was how I found the bulk of my information. I could see the Victory Road girls' football team thread . . . and the boys' . . . *all kinds* of sports teams. I saw the cake recipe Victory Road had planned for the Bake Off. And I saw which choreographer Victory Road had booked, then made sure I pointed Summerby towards the same one."

Grace didn't know what to say. This was mind-blowing.

"He said good journalists always snoop and use their sources," Michael explained, seeing the look on Grace's face. "I don't know, I guess . . . I really wanted to believe that."

Grace nodded. She thought of the moment she reached in Anna's bag to retrieve her private diary, and thought of how blurred the line had seemed between right and wrong, all in the name of ambition.

"I really wanted to win," Michael said. "And I really wanted to help my uncle the way he helped us. But . . . I don't know . . . now it all feels so wrong. I love this park. I don't want it to be destroyed. But it's too late. My uncle's going to build over it and it's all my fault!" he wailed.

Grace put an awkward hand on Michael's shoulder. She'd never seen him like this. He was usually so quiet and composed. Even though he had cheated, and messed up, he seemed *genuinely* sorry. And now that she'd spoken to him, it was easy to see how it had all happened. She *really* wasn't expecting this.

"You probably don't understand." Michael dabbed his eye. "You have loads of friends. But I don't find it easy. Diaz is my only really good mate ... We've known each other since we were little. We used to play here. And now he's going to hate me too."

Grace shook her head. She knew that wasn't true. Diaz would forgive him, *especially* if Michael was willing to do what she asked.

"What if it wasn't too late?" she said.

CHAPTER TWENTY-TWO

SMOOTH STU: We interrupt your Greenfair FM *Smooth Grooves In The Afternoon* With *Smooth Stu* to bring you a special announcement from our Park Protests correspondent ...

MICHAEL: Ladies and gentleman, residents of Greenfair, I know it's been a long day here at the Park Protests, thank you for listening if you've been tuning in from home, but if everyone could please now switch over to Victory Road High School's radio station, *Listen Up!* We promise it will be worth your while ...

Arthur's heart was soaring. He'd been listening to Greenfair FM as he sprinted home. Michael did it! He *actually helped them!* Who knew how Grace had managed this dramatic turn of events, but however she did, it worked! And now more people than ever before would be tuning in to *Listen Up*. With people from all around the neighbourhood – not just the school – listening in, if this came together as they hoped, then it could be their very last chance to save Greenfair Park ...

Arthur was just praying that he'd find his mum, pronto, or all this would have been for nothing.

Finally, Arthur raced up to the path to his front door and hammered on it. "Mum! Mum!" he called. There was no time to let himself in and find her. She had to come *now*.

"Arthur?" His mum opened the door. "What's going on? Is everything all right?"

"It might be," Arthur garbled breathlessly. He explained the situation as quickly as he could.

"Well? Do you think it's enough to stop the developments going ahead?" Arthur was dancing around on the tips of his toes.

"Arthur, love, I'm sorry," his mum said. "I'm in family law – I'm not *totally* clear on the rules around wildlife."

Arthur's heart sank. They needed confirmation *soon*, or everyone would stop listening to *Listen Up*. Grace could only stall for so long.

"But . . ." Arthur's mum added, "I *do* have a colleague who specializes in this sort of thing. She might be able to help us."

Arthur nodded enthusiastically. "Do you think you could speak to her, like, now?"

Arthur's mum folded her arms. "It's a Saturday, so, I shouldn't really . . ."

Arthur couldn't help but show his disappointment. His entire body sagged.

". . . But, she used to live around here, and I'm *sure* she wouldn't mind sparing me a few minutes if it was going to help Greenfair Park."

Arthur jumped up and kissed his mum on the cheek. "ACE!" he yelled. "Mum, you're the best! Come on, let's go, go, go!"

His mum kicked off her slippers and shuffled into her shoes while fumbling for her car keys. They both raced back down the path towards the car.

As soon as they got in, Arthur messaged Kieran to let them know he was on his way. Anna and her Educational whatsit wildlife person – Liane – were already there, which was a relief. Arthur's mum was trying to get through to her colleague on speakerphone, but the line was busy. He turned on *Listen Up*. Grace, Anna and Kieran were playing the interviews they'd recorded earlier, with the townspeople talking about all their favourite memories of Greenfair

Park. Right now it was the man who used to secretly meet his then-girlfriend, now-wife, in the park for moonlit walks under the stars

"Isn't that sweet?" said Arthur's mum.

Arthur nodded, his heart swelling, thinking back over all the many different people who had shown up to defend Greenfair. This is what should have been on the radio today, not all the nonsense about the "stunning industrial chic windows" and "enhanced comfort underfloor heating" in the new flats. But it was better late than never. He only hoped that his mum could reach her colleague, and that they could get back to Greenfair in time.

Grace glanced at the clock. They were surely running out of time before everyone lost faith in their "big announcement". Michael had let them take over the decks and many of the protesters had stayed once they heard the promise of further developments, with a lot of people at home tuning in too. Grace could hardly believe she was broadcasting to *this* many people! It was crazy! But as the minutes ticked by, the numbers were starting to fall. It was the end of the day and no one wanted to listen to beautiful memories of Greenfair now – they were too heartbroken that it was going to be demolished.

Huddled over their microphone, Grace, Kieran and Anna desperately tried to keep up the banter.

"He said, DAM!" Kieran said, as he finished his lame joke. Grace could hear the resounding silence and grimaces slightly. "That's what the . . . fish said when he . . . swam into the big wall . . . yeah . . ."

"Think that joke's *tailing* off a bit," Anna intervened.

"Ha ha," Kieran retorted. "Thanks Anna. I'd be *floundering* without you."

Grace smiled. Anna and Kieran were doing the best they could to keep everyone entertained, but it couldn't go on much longer. Grace received a message from Arthur and rejoiced. He was nearly here! She held up one finger at Kieran and Anna.

"And I know you're all *anxiously waiting* for our special announcement ..." said Grace, her voice cracking under the pressure, "but if you can just bear with us for *one more minute* ..."

They played another of their interviews from earlier as Grace squinted across the park. At last! Arthur was running towards them. Kieran punched the air. Anna started jumping up and down and Grace wiped a droplet of sweat from her forehead.

When Arthur finally reached them, he was well and truly out of breath.

"Well?" Grace cried. "Where's your mum?"

"She's ... over ... there ..." Arthur pointed.

They all looked to where Arthur's mum was on the phone, nodding. "Is that good nodding or bad nodding?" Kieran asked.

"What is a good nod and what is a bad nod?" Anna asked.

Kieran demonstrated, establishing that a "good nod" was basically enthusiastic nodding while looking pleased and "bad nodding" was slow nodding while looking grumpy.

"Hey, hey, what kind of nod is this?" Anna asked. She did a single nod with a blank face.

"Solemn nodding, obvs," Kieran answered.

"Got it in one! YES!" Anna high-fived Kieran.

Arthur was pleased to see Anna and Kieran bonding, but now really *wasn't* the time.

"Ahem, I know we said *one minute* one minute ago, but if you could just give us one more, one more minute . . ." Grace announced.

"Oh, for crying out loud!" One man

in the park called. "I'm leaving. Bunch of dumb kids."

There was a murmur of agreement and lots of people started moving. More and more people were turning off at home, too. This was going *terribly*. Grace was thinking they were just about to lose everyone, when at the very last second, Arthur's mum ended her phone call and came rushing over.

"... I mean, kidding!" Grace improvised. "We're ready for our very special announcement *right this second*. Everybody, joining us today are Environmental Conservation Education and Engagement Officer … er, wildlife expert Liane Fong, and Ms McLean of well-respected law firm, Peterson Law."

Arthur's mum settled into the chair between Grace and Liane. Grace was biting her nails again. Arthur, Kieran and Anna were all holding hands. Depending on what Arthur's mum had found out, this could all go south very quickly. What if the potential great crested newt meant nothing?

"So, ladies and gentlemen, the moment you've all been waiting for . . ." Arthur's voice shook as he leaned in to Kieran's mic. "I'm sure everyone here is familiar with the newts found in Greenfair Park's pond. Liane, can you talk to us a little bit about the different kinds of newts you might find in most ponds?"

A confused murmur rippled through the crowds. Whispers of "This boy's off his trolley!" and "Why is he talking about newts?" could be heard. But Arthur pressed on, handing the mic to Liane.

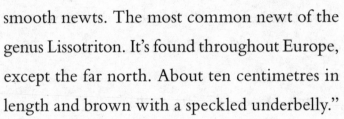

"Sure." Liane took the mic. "So, most newts found in UK ponds are smooth newts. The most common newt of the genus Lissotriton. It's found throughout Europe, except the far north. About ten centimetres in length and brown with a speckled underbelly."

"And can you tell us about great crested newts?"

"Absolutely, great crested news are *much* rarer. Their numbers have been falling drastically since the 1970s, and even though they're just starting to increase again, great crested newts are a protected species in Europe. It can be pretty hard to identify different newts if you don't know what you're looking for, but the most defining feature of the great crested newt is its size. They tend to be a lot bigger, around fifteen to seventeen centimetres as opposed to ten centimetres."

"Amazing," Arthur said. "And can you identify one way or another what kind of newt this is?" He put the picture in front of Liane. "For the benefit of listeners, this newt was discovered in Greenfair park's pond only a few weeks ago."

"This here is *undoubtedly* a great crested newt," Liane confirmed.

There was another wave of whispers amongst the remaining protesters in the park. Kieran gave a thumbs up.

"Incredible, thanks Liane," said Grace. "And now over to you, Ms McLean. We understand you were just on the phone with your colleague, who specializes in environmental law."

"That's right, she's been working in environmental law for twenty years, and she used to live around here, so she's got a very special attachment to Greenfair Park."

"And did she confirm what the discovery of the great crested newt means for Greenfair Park?"

Grace tried so hard to sound neutral, but it was difficult. The atmosphere in the air was tense, and everyone seemed to take a collective breath.

". . . She did." Arthur's mum looked grave for a moment. The group all looked at each other in fear. But then Arthur's mum smiled. "She confirmed, in no uncertain terms, that this discovery complicates the demolition of the park immeasurably. The developers *have* to inform the planning authorities of this new discovery. Additional surveys need to take place and a protected species licence application must be submitted."

For a moment it seemed like there was complete silence. Then everyone in the park seemed to exhale, and a cloud seemed to lift on what had been a miserable day. Grace leaned back in relief and felt the sun on her face. Arthur and Kieran started shaking each other. Anna laughed and hugged her sister. A cheer broke out across the green.

In the crowd, they could see Mr P grabbing his husband, holding him so tightly he picked him up off the ground. Ms Lyall, Roddy and Benjy were jumping around wildly (no one had ever seen Ms Lyall so energetic before) and Tilly-Mae had climbed on Lia's shoulders and had her hands in the air. Grace glanced at Michael, who was grinning from ear to ear as well and looking very, very relieved.

They'd done it. They'd actually done it!

CHAPTER TWENTY-THREE

```
[INTRO: Countdown.

3 ...2 ...1 ...

Roll titles

NEWS PRESENTER: : Hello and welcome to Great
Morning Britain. Your breakfast headlines
today: Hollywood's biggest movie star falls
asleep during his own premiere ... A woman
is charged with stealing half a million US
Dollars' worth of avocados ... And later this
morning we hear about the group of kids who,
against all odds, saved their local park ...
```

Grace, Arthur, Kieran and their families sat in

silence around the TV in Grace's kitchen. They couldn't *believe* the story had been picked up for national broadcast.

Since the interview on *Listen Up*, the council had frozen their permission for Stow Developments to build the block of flats on Greenfair Park. Things had officially come to a standstill!

"Sources say the group of kids, including Grace Best, Arthur McLean, Kieran Summers and Anna Fong," the voice on the TV continued, "discovered the presence of a great crested newt amongst the park's pond life. The great crested newt is a protected species, alongside other creatures such as the pool frog, badgers, bats, dormice, water voles and all kinds of birds and reptiles. Some kids, eh?"

Arthur's mum patted him on the back and his dad whistled. Grace's mum and dad beamed at her. Even Grace's brothers shouted,

"YES, GRACE!"

There was a knock at the door and Grace's mum went to answer it, reentering a moment later with Anna, Lia, Tilly-Mae and Diaz. Anna smiled at Arthur, who immediately started blushing.

"Smooth," whispered Kieran, and Arthur elbowed him.

Their parents shushed them, and they continued to listen to the story. It talked all about their school radio shows and complimented them as "budding young journalists".

"Oh my goodness, I'm so proud!" Grace's mum yelled.

"Now, guys," said Arthur's dad. "First thing you do when you become big radio celebrities is play a *Lad Dadz* track, yeah?" Arthur's parents giggled.

Grace and Arthur laughed along, but they were both feeling pretty overwhelmed by the whole thing. They'd never intended doing this as a way to increase their radio profile; they knew well that some things were more important than that. But inadvertently, they appeared to have become nationwide sensations. Now, kids from schools all across the country were talking about *Radio Royalty, Best of the Best,* and *Anna's Amusings.* Their uploads were getting more plays than ever, and more and more people were tuning in. The ratings for the joint show they had done in the park, interviewing Arthur's mum and Anna's sister, were at least five times higher than any of their previous ratings!

None of them could deny that this was all amazing ... but it was hard to enjoy it, when the park was still technically at risk. The local radio, and now the national news, were reporting as if they had "saved" the park, but in truth, the process had only really hit a bump.

They'd saved it for now, but the flats *could* still go ahead.

Just then, there was another knock at the door. Grace and Arthur frowned at each other, counting everyone around them. They weren't expecting anyone else. Grace's dad went to answer it and came back with Michael.

Everyone stopped what they were doing. Kieran even stopped secretly scoffing all of Grace's mum's chin chin.

"Er," Michael coughed. "I just wanted to come and give you the good news myself. My uncle has decided not to go ahead with the flats."

Everyone's eyes widened. Was Michael serious?

"He didn't get the licence?" Grace queried.

"He, er, he's actually withdrawn his application."

That was definitely *not* what anyone was expecting to hear. They took a moment to let the news sink in. It seemed surreal.

Grace's parents gestured for Michael to sit down.

"When my uncle heard what I'd done," he went on, "I finally came clean with him about how much the park meant to me. He hadn't realized and, given all the additional complications with the great crested newt, he decided it was better for everyone to build the flats somewhere else."

"Well done, Michael!" Arthur cried. "You saved Greenfair Park!"

"No." Michael shook his head. "*You guys* saved it. You spoke up about it and gave me the confidence to do the same."

"Who cares who did what?! The park is saved!" Grace beamed. "Oh my goodness, is this real? Is the park really staying?"

Michael nodded. "It's really staying."

Everyone whooped and clapped. It was

all smiles around the table. They really had saved the day!

"Well, I'll leave you to celebrate," Michael said.

"What? You're going?" Kieran sounded outraged.

"Yeah, stay with us!" Arthur demanded.

"Have some chin chin," Grace added. "If Kieran hasn't eaten them all."

"Are you sure?" Michael asked.

"Sit down, for goodness' sake!" Grace's mum ushered him into a chair, put a plate in front of him, and that was that.

They spent the evening chatting and sharing happy memories of Greenfair Park. It was weird, thought Arthur – they'd been fighting with each other all this time, yet really everyone just wanted the same thing. If they hadn't ended up working *with* Summerby, instead of against them, they wouldn't be here now. Without Anna and Michael, they wouldn't have saved

the park or made national news. (Arthur could still hardly believe it. *National news.*)

Grace looked around the table. Kieran was joking around with serious Michael, who looked like he was already coming out of his shell. Arthur tried to hold Anna's hand but missed and accidentally got sauce on her shirt. Grace caught Anna's eye and they both burst out laughing. With Anna around she felt like she was getting closer to having a proper best girl mate.

Eventually, their new Summerby pals started heading home.

"So . . . friends?" said Michael as they stepped out of the door.

"Ugh, *friends?* With this lot?!" Anna joked. She punched Arthur in the shoulder.

"Yeah, if you wanna call us *friends* then that's fine . . . I guess we can be friends with our *fans*," Arthur retorted.

"Give back to the community and all that,"

Kieran added. He put a hand across his chest and dipped his head forward solemnly.

"Fans? *Fans*?!" Anna squealed. "You've got a thing or two to learn from me, Arthur McLean."

"That's why you write down everything I say in that little notebook, is it?" Arthur teased.

"Whatever, Arthur," Grace interjected. "I saw you scribble down Anna's tips about interview technique on my mum's napkin."

Arthur looked like a child who'd just been caught with his hand in the cookie jar. Grace and Anna high-fived.

"OK, the Summerby versus Victory Road rivalry is still on, then," Michael smiled.

"Yeah, and now you're not winning everything by cheating, watch how we beat you at the next football match." Grace stuck out her hand.

"Challenge accepted," Michael said as

he shook it.

Michael and Anna headed back down the path, already discussing their next pieces of coverage and how to beat Victory Road fairly. For a moment Arthur, Grace and Kieran listened to them, smiling and pulling indignant faces. Now they'd succeeded in saving Greenfair together, they were happy to return to normal with their new friends: it was game on.

LOOK OUT FOR ARTHUR AND
GRACE'S FIRST VICTORY...

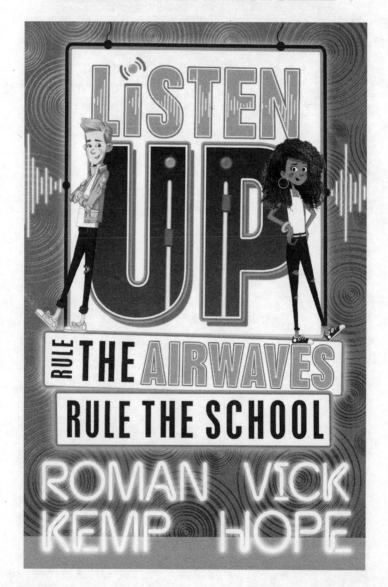

THE THEFT

```
[Intro: Radio Royalty jingle (5 secs).]
ARTHUR: "Listen up, Victory Road! It's the
night of the school's annual chess tournament
and the atmosphere is BUZZING…"
```

The lone sound of someone's laughter echoed round the empty school hall, making Arthur sit up.

"Yeah … no one's going to believe that," said a familiar voice from behind him.

Grace Best. Of course she would be here early too. She stood in front of Arthur with her arms folded across her chest and a patronizing arch in her eyebrow.

"All right," said Arthur. "It's the night of the school's annual chess tournament and the atmosphere is DEAD AS A GRAVEYARD." He laughed at his own joke, but Grace shook her head in mock-pity, making her big, black curls bounce around her shoulders like a hair advert.

"Well *that's* not going to win you any awards for radio journalism, is it?"

She fake-smiled and walked to a seat at the far side of the hall – as far from Arthur as possible – then set down her bag and pulled out a huge book with a chess piece on the front. *Of course she'd done a ton of research for this*, thought Arthur, *and of course she was thinking about awards in radio journalism already*. Grace was always two steps ahead of everyone else, including Arthur. Even her last name was annoyingly smug.

Well, she wasn't going to get the best coverage tonight – Arthur was. But he seriously needed to find a way to make a chess tournament sound fun. Arthur knew Grace would already have her take on the event worked out, but he didn't plan ahead like that. His style was more off the cuff, so inspiration could come from anywhere and ideas always hit him eventually. Although sometimes, like today, they took a little while.

Arthur gulped. What if inspiration *didn't* hit? What if all he had was some boring, standard coverage of a chess tournament?! Arthur shook his head. He wouldn't let Grace Best get in his head! That was exactly what she wanted – to make him nervous so that *Best of the Best* would beat him and his best mate Kieran's radio show, *Radio Royalty*, in the school ratings this week. Theirs were the two most-listened-to shows at Listen Up, the school's radio station. And no matter how hard Arthur and Kieran tried,

Grace was always competing with them for the top spot.

Their styles were quite different. Arthur and Kieran tended to chat with the interviewee and draw them out slowly, whereas Grace was more blunt and straight to the point. But they all desperately wanted the scoop on stuff going on around school.

"Your Highness!" shouted a voice.

"Your Grace!" replied Arthur automatically as he stood up and bowed theatrically to his best mate Kieran, who was standing in the doorway surveying the room like a real king.

This was how they always introduced themselves – in real life and on their show. They fist bumped and sat down next to each other. Arthur felt more relaxed now Kieran was here.

On the other side of the room Grace was trying to read, but the two "kings" whooping in the corner were distracting her. She reached secretively into her bag for one of her mum's puff puffs. OK, so they were delicious, but couldn't her mum ever just give her a Kit-Kat? Her bag was always bulging with huge boxes of Nigerian snacks and it was so embarrassing.

Arthur and Kieran erupted into snorts and Grace finally put down her book. She'd practically become an overnight chess expert, anyway – she even knew all about castling. She

twiddled her thumbs and looked over at the two boys, then quickly away again. *What's it like to have a best mate?* she wondered, with a little pang of jealousy. Grace had friends, but… She sighed. Everyone knew her as "that radio girl". It was kind of like being famous, or that's what she thought. People wanted to hang out with her, but she didn't have any close friends. Arthur and Kieran obviously had a bond – and they obviously had each other's back. Grace wasn't sure if she'd ever find that.

She looked out of the window at the pouring rain. It was unusually rubbish weather, even for winter, and Grace wondered who – apart from her, Arthur and Kieran – was actually going to show up for this. She'd even had doubts about whether she should come, but there was no way she'd let *Radio Royalty* get a possible scoop over *Best of the Best*. As the thoughts turned over in her mind, the doors opened and a surprising number of kids started schlepping in.

With some in twos and some in groups, they noisily filled up the hall. Grace caught Arthur's eye.

"Told you, Bestie, BUZZING!' he shouted, and he did a victory dance. Grace rolled her eyes and the kids still walking in looked between them in amusement; their rivalry was well known around school.

Well, she had to admit it: Arthur was right. The atmosphere *was* buzzing.

As everyone took their seats, the chess-players began filing on to the stage. The first to walk out were the Klimach sisters, Nikita and Misha, instantly recognizable by their long, dark hair and pale skin. They were practically identical and wore similarly determined, narrow-eyed expressions, but Nikita was older than Misha. They'd been winning chess tournaments together since they were really young. Next out was Jordan Baptiste, with his locks and cool shoes. Jordan acted like an old man trapped in a twelve-year-old's body – he was always contemplating the meaning of life. Next came a small, blinking, dark-haired first year called Bea Shaffi. Grace had found her lost in the corridors on a couple of occasions and she seemed like a sweet kid. She was closely followed by Roddy Lyall, who was the headmistress's son, and her spitting image with red hair and freckles. Everyone called Bea a chess prodigy, but Roddy... Well, Ms Lyall entered him for everything, whether he wanted to compete or not. They were the youngest contestants and they both looked petrified.

In the hall, Arthur nudged Kieran and pointed over at Alan, the school caretaker, who had entered from the right hand door by the stage, carrying a large, gleaming trophy.

Their slightly scary headmistress Ms Lyall, who was sitting right at the front with Roddy's little brother and the rest of the contestants' families, got up to introduce the competition. She stood at the front of the stage, right by the trophy.

"Welcome," she boomed, "to the tenth annual Victory Road chess tournament. This year we've got a wealth of talent – old and new – competing, and I wish every contestant the very best of luck. So without further ado, let the games begin!"

She gestured towards the trophy and the hall burst into applause.

Bea's eyes brightened, Roddy fidgeted in his seat, Nikita and Misha's eyes seemed to go even narrower and even Jordan looked full of determination as Alan sat the trophy in the middle of the stage, in all its glory.

Grace braced herself. Maybe this was going to be more interesting than she'd thought.

Or maybe not. One hour later, Grace was

trying to concentrate on the game, but it was hard. None of her books had mentioned that chess was this S L O W.

The first few rounds had been OK. They were quick-fire chess, which meant the opponents had to move every ten seconds. Arthur had been in his element, bopping around yelling, "Ouch, that's gotta hurt!" when a piece got knocked over or, "Ooh, that was below the belt!" and doing dramatic countdowns in the players' ears. At one point, Roddy was so alarmed by him that he accidentally won. The crowd had broken into raucous laughter and Arthur had given a bow. Even Grace had to admit it was funny.

But now they were down to the semi-finals, there were no time limits on the games, which meant the remaining players were really

taking

their

time.

Despite his accidental win, Roddy had been swiftly eliminated in the quick-fire rounds and sat awkwardly on a bench by the side of the stage. So now it was down to Bea and Nikita, and Jordan and Misha. It felt like time was standing still. Grace was *sure* the clock had stopped moving. And by the looks of things, they still had quite a long game to get through. People were starting to shuffle in their seats and stare out the window. Even Arthur seemed to have run out of jokes. The only sound was the rain beating on the roof, and the deep rumbling of thunder.

Come on, pay attention, Grace thought to herself. *Radio Royalty* had been outdoing her this evening, but this was her moment. While Arthur and Kieran had been focusing on the individual games, Grace had been uncovering the history between the players.

The elusive Klimach sisters were supposedly

unbeatable; they had *never* lost a game in the school's chess tournament history. But this year was different: they usually played as a team, but tonight they might play against each other.

Bea was an underdog because of her age, but could she become the first person ever to beat the Klimach sisters, and the youngest winner of the chess tournament *ever?*

Or would it be Jordan, who was currently playing the oldest Klimach sister, Nikita. She had beat him to the coveted science prize – had he been practising day and night to ensure his trophy, and his revenge?!

Now that *sounds interesting,* Grace thought to herself with a smile. And she'd wait for exactly the right moment to liven things up.